YOUNG BLOOD

Also in this series

Big Deal (2)

DAVID ROSS AND BOB CATTELL

CARLTON

THIS IS A CARLTON BOOK

This edition published in 2010 by Carlton Books Limited
A division of the Carlton Publishing Group
20 Mortimer Street, London W1T 3JW

First published in 1999 by André Deutsch

A catalogue record for this book is available from the British Library.

1 3 5 7 9 10 8 6 4 2

ISBN: 978-1-84732-490-0

Printed in the UK by CPI Mackays, Chatham, ME5 8TD

Bob Cattell was born in the Fens and now lives in Suffolk. He combines his job as a copywriter with writing children's books about football and cricket – including the Glory Gardens series. He is a lifelong Aston Villa supporter.

David Ross was somehow always the reserve in his school football team, which gave him lots of time to observe the game. He loves to hate supporting Heart of Midlothian and has written numerous other books for children.

CHAPTER ONE

BACK IN THE SQUAD

'Righto, laddie. Get out there and show us what you can do,' said Len Dallal.

They were the words Thomas had been longing to hear for weeks. A whole month out of the first team with a torn hamstring had been bad enough. But the three weeks which followed, when he had been in the reserves wondering whether the boss had forgotten about him, had been the complete pits.

His first season with Sherwood Strikers had begun like a fairy tale. He'd scored a goal after five minutes in his opening league game with 'the greatest club in the world', and another in his second appearance. Suddenly he was the wonder kid of the Premier League. The press had gone wild. The sports pages were crammed with pictures of 'Young Thomas Headley – player of the month'. 'The brightest of all the great Sherwood Strikers' young stars' the *Post* said, and his phone never stopped ringing with requests for interviews and TV appearances. Then he had got injured and everyone had seemed to have forgotten him.

'The boss says you slot into the midfield on the left,' said Len. 'So Skip switches to the centre. Understood?'

Thomas nodded. Len Dallal – better known as 'Doolally' – was Strikers' senior coach. He was ancient and quite mad but all the players respected him because he was the best reader of the game in the Premier League and probably in the world. He'd had loads of offers to go abroad but he always said it wasn't natural to leave England. Old Doolally could be a bit odd; Thomas had learned to watch out for his unpredictable moods. But the truth was that there was only one thing in Len's life – football. Even Thomas couldn't imagine what it was like to be as obsessed about the game as Len was. You never saw him wearing anything else but a Sherwood Strikers track suit; Ashleigh Coltrane said he even slept in it. And his house was painted Sherwood colours: red and white – inside and out.

'Get down the wing and put in some deep crosses,' said Len. 'But if you get a chance, nip inside and run at the defence. Use your speed. A free kick just outside the box and we might nick it with a set-piece.' Len gave Thomas a big slap on the back as he ran out on to the pitch.

Thomas glanced up at the big screen. There were just nine minutes of extra time left to play and the scoreboard read:

Sherwood Strikers 1	**Highfield Rovers 1**
Coltrane (88)	Burger (15 o.g.)

All right, it was only the quarter-final of the League Cup and a lot of the big clubs didn't take the competition too seriously these days. But it still offered qualification for Europe for the winners and, more important still, Sherwood never liked being beaten by Highfield Rovers. Besides, the boss always said, 'Play to win every time – that way you get the winning habit.' It was good advice.

The first leg against Rovers had also finished 1–1 – so, after 200 minutes of football, there was still nothing to separate the two teams. Ashleigh Coltrane had scrambled tonight's equalizer in the dying minutes of normal time. Now they were into extra time and if the scoreline stayed the same the game would go to penalties.

One of the loudest cheers of the evening greeted Thomas as the official held up his number – number seven. A song rose above the cheers:

'We all agree
Tommy is better than Deekie'

Graham Deek, Highfield Rovers' own rising star and a year older than Thomas, was already in the England B squad at the age of 18. The football press had all run stories about the two of them; the stars of the future, they called them and, in the eyes of the world, Headley and Deek were locked in a deadly battle for a midfield place in the England team for next year's World Cup. In fact, Thomas had known Deekie for years, they'd played together as England juniors and they were the best of mates, sharing a room several times on tour with the Young England set-up.

Thomas replaced Frankie Burger in midfield. As they crossed Thomas held out his hand for the usual friendly touch. Frankie ran past without even looking at him. He looked furious and disappeared straight up the tunnel – ignoring the management and players on the bench. He probably wasn't too happy about that own goal, thought Thomas.

Thomas's first touch of the ball was nearly his last. He picked up a pass down the wing from Ben El Harra and beat one defender but the centre back came across and clattered him and the ball into the advertising hoarding. Thomas fell awkwardly with his right leg bent under him. It was an ugly foul and it earned the Highfield player a yellow card and a torrent of abuse from the crowd. Thomas got to his feet very gingerly, terrified that he might have another serious injury; but everything seemed okay and he soon ran off the slight pain in his knee.

With less than five minutes to go, Ashleigh Coltrane, Sherwood's top goalscorer, hit the crossbar. From the rebound Highfield broke quickly and a low cross from their winger was met by Graham Deek diving forward. It looked a goal from the moment he made contact. But Sean

Pincher in the Strikers goal reacted like a cat. He took off, back arched, left arm at full stretch. Somehow, just as the ball looked certain to bury itself in the top right-hand corner of the net he got his fingertips to it. There was a gasp from the crowd behind the goal as the ball flashed upwards, hit the crossbar and deflected over.

'Pincher, Pincher,' roared the crowd behind the goal. At last they were really getting behind Sherwood. It had been a strangely subdued performance up till then. The Reds' supporters didn't like their team losing and they were quick to show their disapproval when things went wrong.

Sherwood and Rovers were one minute away from a penalty shoot-out when Thomas took a nicely weighted long pass from Dean Oldie on his chest halfway inside the Rovers half. He turned the defender who was marking him tightly and two other Highfield players immediately blocked his route to goal. Thomas feinted to go down the wing and then cut inside, pushing the ball past the first sliding tackle and jumping over the defender's legs. Only the centre back stood between him and the goal. To his right Ashleigh Coltrane was free and calling for the ball. But Thomas decided to go it alone. He ran straight at the defender, dummied to go left and then went round him on the right. But, as he fought for his balance before he could shoot at goal, he felt the tug at his shirt and his feet went from under him.

The ref had seen it too. And the red card was

his only option. The big defender didn't go quietly. He swung a punch at Ashleigh Coltrane who ducked just in time and, in the end, he had to be escorted off the pitch by his team-mates. The free kick was on the edge of the area and by the time Highfield had lined up their wall, extra time was almost over. Jamie MacLachlan, Sherwood's skipper, took charge. The set-pieces had all been rehearsed a thousand times on the practice ground.

'Fourteen,' said Jamie. All the set-pieces were numbered – and, as the players took up their positions, Ashleigh Coltrane gave Thomas a nudge. 'Great run,' he said. 'But next time you see me free, pass the damn ball, okay?'

'But you hit the crossbar last time,' said Thomas with a smile. 'I didn't think I could risk it.'

Ashleigh grinned fiercely. 'Right, you just watch me, man.'

Jamie and Cosimo Lagattello, the dead-ball specialist, lined up behind the ball which was placed just inside the D.

'Maybe isa more good when I heet it forte,' said Cosimo, whose English hadn't improved much since his arrival from Italy.

'Mebee ya didna hair me,' said Jamie. 'Number 14, ya ken?'

Cozzie looked a bit wounded. 'Capisco bene. I understanda right,' he said. For some reason he seemed to understand Big Mac's broad Scottish accent better than most other forms of English.

The ref blew his whistle and Jamie ran in, dummied a floated pass to the far post and ran over the ball. Cosimo followed rapidly behind him and Thomas and Kevin Wardle began their runs, drawing off two of the defenders. Highfield were probably still betting on a curled shot over the wall when Cosimo stopped and chipped a pass to the feet of Ashleigh who had lost his marker and was coming in at full speed toward the near post. He met the ball on the volley and, as the goalie came out, he buried it low and hard.

It was the perfect finish and the crowd leapt to salute the scorer. Ashleigh ran to the touchline pursued by the other forwards. Then he stopped, stared at the crowd with his hands on his hips for a second and finally gave them his trademark, the Coltrane shuffle. His arms pumped up and down like a steam train as he limboed back until his head nearly touched the ground. By then Thomas and the others had caught up with him and, as Ashleigh was buried under a pile of red shirts, the referee blew for the end of the game.

2–1 on the night. Sherwood Strikers were through to the semi-finals of the League Cup – 3–2 on aggregate.

Len Dallal and the boss, Joss Morecombe, walked onto the pitch from the dug-out to salute the crowd and the players. Joss had been the Reds' manager for four years. In the eight seasons before his arrival the great club hadn't won a trophy. It had been the leanest spell in the Strikers history; things had got so bad that they had nearly been relegated from the Premier League. In his first season with the club Joss had won them the FA Cup. For a time that made him a hero but the Premier League title still eluded him. The closest Sherwood had come to the old glory days had been third last season. And that wasn't good enough for some of the fans. They dreamed of one thing only – being the top club in the world again. So, two months into the season and with Strikers only just above halfway in the league, there were already calls from a small but growing faction of the supporters for Joss to go.

Thomas liked Joss. You knew where you stood with him. When Thomas had signed from Newlynn City in the late spring of last year, the boss had gone out of his way to look after him and help him to settle down in Sherwood. It was the first time that Thomas had lived away from home and Joss had not only helped him find a flat, he'd also protected him from the pressures of the press and the fans. He was a big man with receding white hair which was swept back over his collar. His face creased easily and regularly into a broad smile which made him look like everyone's favourite uncle. But behind that smile was the quickest and shrewdest mind in football management. And he was tough too, he needed to be.

There was a chorus of 'Out, out, out,' and a few boos from a small section of the ground as Joss walked onto the pitch but he didn't appear to notice and he waved and smiled as usual. Most of the crowd gave him the reception you'd expect after a good Cup win, even though it had gone to the final minute. Joss walked up to Jamie MacLachlan who was making his way to the tunnel with Thomas.

'You and Ashleigh can do the telly interview, Mac,' he said to Jamie. 'Make sure you say nice things about me.' Then he turned to Thomas and said, 'Well played, Thomas, lad. I thought you were looking quite sharp. The telly boys want to interview you too but I told them you were busy. If you're not rushing off I wouldn't mind a chat with you after you've showered. See you in the room in half an hour eh?'

Thomas nodded. What could Joss want? But before he could give it much thought he was surrounded by a group of young autograph hunters who all wanted their '7 Headley' shirts signed by their latest hero.

CHAPTER TWO

YOUTH CLUB

Joss Morecombe's office was just behind the East Stand at the Park End of Strikers' ground. For a top Premier League club it wasn't the smartest manager's office – Joss liked things to be 'comfortable', which meant his 'room', as he called it, was more like a store cupboard than an executive suite. It was full of old armchairs, and cardboard boxes stacked in great piles that all looked as if they were about to topple over and bury someone. Pictures of players past and present lined the walls, including one of Joss in his playing days with St James, wearing very tight shorts.

'Pull up a pew, lad,' said Joss, pointing to a stack of chairs in the corner. Thomas picked one up and placed it in front of Joss's desk. ''Spect you're wondering why I asked you here.' Joss wasn't one to waste time with words; he usually got straight to the point.

'Is it about the game? Did I play okay?' asked Thomas nervously.

'I thought you had a smashing ten minutes. Put yourself about, even showed a bit of class. I only wish I'd brought you on sooner. How's the hammy?'

Thomas felt the hamstring at the back of his right leg. 'Fine. But I'm seeing the physio tomorrow in case there's any reaction.'

'Good. Well actually, son, I haven't asked you here to ask after your health. What I want to know is whether you're ready for the big role I've got in mind for you. I've talked to the skipper and he thinks you'll be up for it. But what about you?'

'Big role?'

Joss laughed. 'Sorry I haven't told you yet, have I? Well . . . It's no secret we're not getting the results we should be this season – especially in the Premier League. It's not shortage of talent that's holding us back – I'd say we've got the strongest squad we've ever had. Ought to have with the money we've been spending. But there are one or two players – and you'll have to work out who they are for yourself – who aren't sticking their chests out when they pull on a red shirt. And Joss Morecombe can only work with players who give 120 per cent.'

Joss gave him a searching look and Thomas wondered who he was talking about. Frankie Burger probably – he'd been pretty impossible on the practice ground lately. But who else? Kevin Wardle, maybe? The number ten had been badly out of form for a few weeks. Cosimo? Strikers' Italian star had cost £18 million from Lazio last season and he'd never quite been at home in the English game. There was no question that he was a genius, but there were times when it would have been good to see a bit less genius and a bit more work. But Cozzie was lazy – and no one seemed to be able to change that.

Joss continued, 'So, in the next couple of weeks you're all going to see some big changes at Trent Park. We've got some good young'uns coming up from the youth team and I'm going to give some of them a chance to prove themselves at top level – sooner rather than later.'

Thomas looked Joss squarely in the eyes but he didn't say a word.

'There's your mate, Jason, for instance. And young Drew Stilton,' said Joss. 'Now I can tell from your face that you don't think much of the lad Drew and you're right – he's an arrogant little swine. But he's skilful and he's quick – and it takes all sorts to make up a football team.'

'He's all right,' said Thomas without much enthusiasm. Arrogant wasn't the word for Drew Stilton. Flash, ignorant and brain-dead were more like it. But Thomas couldn't argue about his skills. Touch, ball control, pace . . . Drew certainly had all the talent in the world. Only trouble was that he thought he was already up with the greats – if not the greatest player the world had ever seen. Jason Le Braz had plenty of talent too, but you never heard him bragging about what a star he was. Jason and Thomas had been good friends from the day Thomas arrived at Trent Park. Along with Rory Betts, the reserve goalkeeper, Jason was probably his best mate amongst the playing staff; the three of them protected each other against the fans and the media and they saw a lot of each other . . . going to films and clubs together – though Thomas was never as keen on clubbing as Jason and Rory, probably because he didn't drink and wasn't that mad about dancing.

'So what you're wondering is, why am I telling you all this?' said Joss.

'I suppose so.'

'Pressure. Simple as that.'

'Pressure?'

'Yes. Can you handle it? If we go with three teenagers in the team and don't get the results, then the media boys are going to be down on us like a herd of elephants. Now Drew and Jason came up through the Sherwood system. They didn't cost us anything. But the press think we paid a packet for you. Fact is, £6 million is nothing these days and I know St James were about to bid twice as much for you, and Barbican were after you too – so we got you for a song. But the press don't know that, do they?'

Thomas blinked. It was the first he'd heard of St James being interested in him. Still, that didn't worry him. Sherwood was where he wanted to be. It was a big set-up with more fans and probably more money than any other team in the Premier League. He knew Sherwood Strikers offered him the best chance of attracting the attention of the England management. And that's what he wanted.

'So, if I experiment with a young squad,' continued Joss, 'and we don't get the results immediately, those so-called journalists will come snarling around. They'll be looking for me all right but they'll give you a tough time too – you can count on that. And, like I said, can you take it?'

'I guess so.'

'You'll have to do better than that. I'm counting on you. With your experience you can help us bring young Jason and Drew along. It's a big step up from the youth side or the reserves, and you've got the match experience to give them a hand up even though you're a few months younger than both of them. Keep an eye on them; talk them through the tough times. As for the hatchet boys from the press, all you need to do is prepare yourself for the worst. The best advice I can give you is to go and talk about it to that business manager of yours. She'll sort it for you.' Joss winked. He meant, of course, Thomas's mum, Elaine.

When Thomas had arrived at Sherwood Strikers he'd been besieged by offers from agents to look after his business affairs. At his previous club, second division Newlynn City, he'd relied on Elaine to handle all the business side for him – after all she was a restaurant manager, so she knew all about contracts and stuff like that. Thomas had been at the Premier League club for about a month and was beginning to feel a bit isolated when Elaine had the idea of becoming his full-time manager. It was the perfect solution. She gave up her job and the whole family moved to Sherwood. It suited Thomas just fine. Elaine – as he always called her, never mum – took over as his manager and Thomas moved out of his flat and back home again into their new family home close to the Trent Park ground.

'I'll have a word with her,' said Thomas.

'Then I'll be hearing from Elaine,' said Joss with a smile. She never hesitated to call Joss when she felt he needed to hear her opinion, and he liked the way she handled things and admired her honest, straight-down-the-line approach to things. 'You can tell her about this too.' He pressed a sheet of paper into Thomas's hand. 'It's Saturday's team.'

1
Sean Pincher

2 Dave Franchi — 4 Brad Trainor — 5 Dean Oldie — 3 Ben El Harra

8 Cosimo Lagattello — 6 Jamie MacLachlan — 7 Thomas Headley

20 Drew Stilton — 9 Ashleigh Coltrane — 21 Jason Le Braz

Reserves:
22 Rory Betts; 14 Tarquin Kelly; 15 Boris Poniowski; 18 Curtis Cropper

'But you've dropped Haile Reifer and. . .' began Thomas.

'And Wardle and Burger,' Joss nodded. 'Haile's picked up a nasty knee niggle in training – could be a ligament problem. The other two are, well – just resting.'

Thomas looked at the team sheet again. He could see that this was dynamite. He was already starting to imagine the reaction in the dressing room.

'Like I said, talk to your mother about it,' said Joss. 'Otherwise keep your mouth shut. I'm not announcing the squad for the Mersey City game until Friday morning and I don't want the hacks besieging my office all week.'

Thomas's little brother Richie was lying in wait for him when he got home.

'You played okay, I suppose,' said Richie leaping out before Thomas was quite through the front door. 'But Deekie was right unlucky, wasn't he? He should have had a hat trick.' Richie Headley had been at Trent Park for the game – he never missed a chance to see his brother play and he worshipped the ground he walked on. At school he never stopped being questioned about his famous brother; the girls all wanted signed photos of Thomas and Richie could have made a fortune out of them if he'd wanted to.

But there was one problem. Richie was a Highfield Rovers fan and nothing, absolutely nothing, would make him give up supporting

Rovers. Just because Thomas had made the big mistake of signing for Strikers didn't mean that he, Richie, had to turn his back on the team he'd dreamed of playing for all his life. Richie was just twelve but already people were saying that he was going to be a better footballer than his brother.

'I'm in the team for Saturday,' said Thomas.

'That's against Mersey City away, isn't it? Can I come?'

'Ask Elaine. You can even come free on the team coach if you'll change your mind about being our mascot.'

'Me a Sherwood Strikers mascot? You must be joking – I support Rovers – not the Reds.'

'Then why don't you go and watch Rovers instead? What did you think of Ashleigh's goal, by the way?' said Thomas, ruffling his little brother's hair.

'Think I'll go to bed,' said Richie glumly, reflecting again on his team's defeat.

'Where's Elaine?'

'Watching telly. You just missed the highlights. Jamie MacLachlan said you clinched the game with your last-minute run. I thought that was a bit generous.'

'Oh, did you, now?'

'Yeah, and I saw Len Dallal at the ground,' continued Richie. 'He's completely nuts.'

'Yeah? Tell me another.'

'He came over just to tell me that he'd bought a new pair of boots – Marauders they're called. He told me all about them: "Nice sunny day, you'll never find a better boot, laddie; bit of frost, Marauders is what you want. Just great they are – nothing better. But, if it's been raining, stick to your old boots or you'll be sliding around on your bum all day." Funny that, eh?'

Thomas laughed at his brother's convincing take-off of Len. 'That sounds like Doolally all right. So I suppose you want me to get you a pair of – what do you call them?'

'Marauders. Will you?'

'If you stop supporting Rovers.'

'Never.'

'Then I'll buy you a pair if you go to bed.'

'I heard Frankie Burger's on the transfer list.'

'Who told you that?'

'That's for you to find out,' said Richie, ducking under his brother's arm and disappearing up the stairs. 'Oh and that journalist rang. What's her name? That one from the *Mirror* with the posh voice. I think she fancies you.'

At that moment the phone rang and Thomas picked it up. 'Thomas, is that you? It's Katie.'

Katie Moncrieff was a sports journalist on the *Mirror*. She was probably the only football writer Thomas trusted – although Elaine told him he should not trust any of them because it was their job to get a story at all costs, and that's all any of them thought about. Katie was quite a bit older than Thomas – maybe twenty-two or twenty-three. She was pretty, very easy to talk to and she certainly knew her stuff on football.

'Listen, Thomas,' she began, 'I've been hearing some strange rumours today. Did you know Frankie Burger's on the transfer list?'

'Sort of,' said Thomas, trying to sound vague.

'And he had a punch-up tonight with Jamie MacLachlan.'

'I didn't know that.'

'Well, it might not be true. That creep Barney Haggard from Sherwood FM told me. But that's not why I'm ringing. There's something else. Something important – and I can't talk to you about it on the phone. When can I see you? Are you playing Saturday?'

Something in Katie's voice made Thomas think this was serious. Forgetting Joss's orders about keeping the team a secret he said, 'Yes, I'm playing. I could see you after the game if you like . . . I'll meet you outside the players' bar.'

'Great. Well played, by the way. You should have come on earlier.'

'Thanks.'

Thomas put the phone down slowly. That was twice in two minutes he'd heard about Frankie Burger being transferred; after what the boss had told him, there could well be some truth in it. Frankie had been with the Reds for five seasons, but his form had been in decline lately and the worse it got the more difficult he'd become. Frankie wasn't the brightest in the team . . . to be honest he was so stupid you almost felt sorry for him. The trouble was that he couldn't handle success or failure. When things went well he'd show off and strut about like a peacock; the bad times just made him morose and bad-tempered. It probably didn't help that Frankie's brother Dez ran one of the most successful business empires in the area. He was so clever and smart that you could imagine that Frankie had felt inferior all his life.

'Who was that on the phone?' asked his mother as Thomas stalked into the sitting room. Thomas told her and then launched into the story of his chat with Joss Morecombe. Elaine Headley listened attentively. She was much smaller than Thomas but she was slim with an alert look, and scarcely seemed old enough to be his mother.

When he had finished his story she thought for a moment and then spoke in her gentle West Indian accent, 'Hmmm. Whatever's that Joss Morecombe up to now? Maybe I'll call in tomorrow and find out.'

'I think he's kind of expecting you,' said Thomas.

'Don't you go talking about this to Katie Moncrieff or any of those other journalists now,' said Elaine, wagging her finger at him.

'Of course I won't.'

Elaine's features softened into a broad smile. 'Well, it's what you want, isn't it? A regular first-team place?' she asked.

'It'll mean more money, too,' said Thomas.

'Don't you worry about money. That's my job and I'm not going to let it spoil you.' Elaine suddenly looked very serious. 'How many boys your age, do you think, earn over £20,000 a week, Thomas?'

'Not many. Why?'

'Because you can't earn wages like that without it having an effect on you. People will treat you differently for a start. And there'll be a lot of chancers and flatterers and crooks trying to get into your life and get a piece of the action.'

'Are you complaining about the money?'

'Not a bit. You're a brilliant footballer and, if you play to your ability, you're probably worth twice your salary and transfer fee to Strikers. But remember what I say. Watch out for the freeloaders. And don't let it spoil you.' Elaine put on her glasses and peered down at the big diary on her knee. 'Now you've got two engagements this week. Tuesday you're opening the new multiplex cinema in town with Ashleigh Coltrane and on Thursday you've got a modelling engagement with *Upfront* magazine.'

'Modelling?'

'It's their men's spring fashion feature. I've seen the clothes – they're nice. They'll suit you.' Elaine chuckled to herself.

'But I thought you said I earned too much money. I don't mind the modelling but opening things is boring.'

'It's not the money. It's your image. And you'll just have to trust me that I know about these things. You've got two charity events next week and there's no money in either of them.'

'That reminds me, Big Mac wants me to do a

football match for Children in Need next month. His eleven against a showbiz team.'

'That's fine. I'll talk to him about it. Now you get to bed. I don't want you getting too knackered to earn your living.' Elaine smiled at her son. 'I'm really glad you're back in the team, Thomas. And Jason will be happy too. Just remember you're picked on merit and, if you play your best, no man can criticize you.'

'Try telling that to Frankie Burger.'

'It's no fault of yours that Frankie has been dropped. If you have any trouble from him, just you let me know. He'll think twice before taking me on.'

Too true, thought Thomas. Then his thoughts drifted back to the conversation with Katie. What was her big secret? Was it to do with Sherwood Strikers? He'd just have to wait till Saturday to find out.

CHAPTER THREE

DOUBLE CROSS

Home games at Trent Park, Strikers' 55,000-seat stadium, were always a sell-out. It was probably the most glamorous venue in the Premier League and certainly the noisiest. But the team's following ensured that away games were something special too. Over 10,000 supporters from all over the country would converge on these games and often the Strikers' fans outnumbered the home team's support.

That wasn't quite true today. Mersey City was a big club too. They were third in the Premier League, eight places above Sherwood, and they had won the title last season. As usual it was a sell-out and the crowd was enormous; Sherwood's coach needed a police escort to reach the ground. Inside the stadium there was a buzz of anticipation.

Just before the game Thomas had a brief word with Jamie MacLachlan, the Reds' captain. Jamie, known to the players as 'Mac' or 'Big Mac' to distinguish him from the club's other Mac –

Lanny 'Little Mac' McEwan – had done everything in the game and there was no one in the entire team Thomas respected more. He'd been at Mersey City with Joss Morecombe and followed him when Joss got the Strikers job. Jamie had three FA Cup winner's medals and he'd won every other title and trophy going, including the Premier League with City. Every title, that is, except the European Champions League – Jamie badly wanted to win that one. He'd also played loads of games for Scotland and captained them in the last World Cup.

The only trouble with Mac – at least for Thomas – was making sense of anything he said. Jamie's accent was more or less impenetrable. Jason Le Braz said it was easier to understand Cozzie Lagattello speaking Italian than Jamie speaking English, and Thomas thought so too.

So when Jamie spoke Thomas listened hard. He couldn't hope to catch every word but he somehow worked out that most of it was about the tactics for the game. It helped that they'd already been through it all several times with Doolally on Friday at the practice ground. Ashleigh Coltrane was to play the lone target role with Jason, Drew dropping off him and the midfield supporting on the break. It was a typical away game defensive plan. Mac went on to say – or so Thomas guessed – that Mersey City would be tough opposition, especially with Strikers putting out half their youth team and having a totally new formation up front. He told Thomas to watch out for Nicky

Clegg who would probably be marking him – everyone knew Clogger was one of the hard men of the game.

Thomas was beginning to think he'd at last cracked the Scottish accent when Jamie said, 'A' richt, laddie. Ya cannae dae better than gie yer best. And ya keep yer heed aboot ya weel fa a wean. But I'm nae shure aboot tha Steelton laddie – thon's a cocky wee booger.'

Thomas nodded and then shook his head slightly to give Mac the impression that he'd understood. He was almost grateful, for once, to be interrupted by Drew Stilton.

'The boss wants you both in the dressing room – time for his little warm-up talk. Waste of time if you ask me. I'd rather do my warming up on the pitch.' If Drew was nervous about his first game for Sherwood Strikers he certainly wasn't showing it.

'I told that girl from the *Mirror* I'd score before half time, so you'd better give me something to get on the end of,' said Drew to Thomas.

'Don't forget that Ashleigh's the front man – we're supposed to be playing off him,' said Thomas.

'Do leave off, mate. Ashleigh Coltrane, Ashleigh Coltrane – that's all I ever hear at this club. I tell you I'm going to score more goals than Mr brilliant Coltrane. Then we'll see who's the real star of Sherwood Strikers.'

'You've got a bit of catching up – Ashleigh's already got ten league goals this season.'

'That's cool. He's going to need a ten–nil start on me. You'll see.'

Joss's pep talk was more or less a further repeat of what Doolally had said on Friday. Tackle back, get behind the ball but don't get too compressed at the back, plenty of support on the break for Ashleigh and watch out for the super-efficient Mersey City offside trap.

City, third in the league behind St James and West Thames Wanderers, had only lost one home game all season and their defensive record was the best in the Premier League. No one was underestimating the task ahead – except perhaps Drew Stilton, who was already talking about his first league hat-trick.

When the Strikers team was announced to the crowd just before kick-off, there were a few cheers from the away fans and jeers from the City supporters at the news that Haile, Kevin and Frankie – all of whom appeared in the programme – had been replaced in the line-up by Thomas, Drew and Jason. A couple of the morning papers had leaked the news, so it wasn't the big surprise that it might have been. But there was a lot of talk about what was going on at Strikers.

Sherwood ran out onto the pitch to chants of 'Big Mac! Where's Burger?' and 'Darling, we're the Young Ones' from the home supporters.

The first half was a bit boring – not pretty to watch but it went to plan. The Sherwood players got behind the ball and didn't give City much room. Thomas was closely marked by Clogger who knew how to use his elbows in a tackle and once he went over the top of the ball and caught Thomas high on the shin. The foul deserved a yellow card but the ref only gave a free kick. Dean Oldie got the only yellow card of the half for a late tackle on their number eight. The only other notable events of the half were a couple of good breaks both wasted by Drew Stilton getting caught offside. At half time Ashleigh had a sharp word with him.

'If I'm the lone striker, how come you keep getting called offside?' he said.

'I guess it's because the midfield's too slow putting me through,' said Drew with a shrug.

'Listen, stupid,' said Ashleigh with more than a trace of irritation. 'If I'm the front man you pull back and link up with the guys behind. Understood?'

'Okay by me' said Drew with a sneer. He made a V sign behind Ashleigh's back as he walked away.

Strikers went 1–0 down to a soft goal right at the beginning of the second half. A weak clearance by Dave Franchi fell at the feet of their skipper and Brad Trainor slipped going in to block the first-time shot. Sean Pincher was probably unsighted in goal as he mistimed his dive and the ball slipped in under his body.

Immediately after that, the City fans were cheering again when Dean Oldie was sent off for a second offence. The tackle on Clogger Clegg was late all right, but Clogger had been handing out a lot of cynical stuff and most players would have been given the benefit of the doubt. Dean's reputation got him into a lot of trouble however, and refs tended to book him automatically – there was something about his attitude that simply asked for a yellow card. It was his third sending off this season.

1–0 down with ten men; things were not looking good for Sherwood. Big Mac went back to plug the hole in the defence, Jason went to play on the left of midfield, and Thomas moved to the centre. For a period of twenty minutes the ball was hardly out of the Strikers half. Then Ashleigh Coltrane got on the end of a long through pass out of defence, turned his marker and cut outside onto the wing. With two players blocking his route to goal, he held up the ball long enough for Jason and Drew to get up in support and then he broke down the wing to the dead-ball line. A perfect, curling cross came over and Jason got to it ahead of the City full back. There wasn't much power in his header but the goalie chose to punch it clear instead of holding it and the ball looped out into the path of Thomas.

From just inside the penalty area Thomas hit it first time on the volley – his body well over the ball. He knew instantly that it was a sweet strike. His hand was raised before the ball streaked past the keeper. There was a massive groan from the City crowd behind the goal as they watched the net balloon under the power of the shot. Thomas stood for a split second and then ran towards the far end of the ground to salute the Strikers' supporters. He'd not made twenty yards before he was dragged to the ground by Jason and Ashleigh and then buried under half the Sherwood team. In his moment of triumph he hardly noticed that his nose was being squashed into the turf.

1–1. Sherwood still had a lot of defending to do, but the ten players held on gamely until the final whistle. 1–1 away – that was a good result against any team in the Premier League – but against City it was outstanding. Big Mac was delighted. He gave Thomas a hearty thump on the back at the end of the game as they disappeared up the tunnel.'Gie's a gaem or twa, Tommeh an we'al ha' a team tae mak'em a' turn doulie.' Thomas nodded sagely and trotted on.

It was a better result than anyone had dared to expect from the new line-up and even the solitary point took a little bit of pressure off Strikers.

The main topic in the dressing room after was Thomas's goal. 'Headlines tomorrow, Tommy,' said Ashleigh. 'Any guesses what they'll say?'

' "Deadly Headley",' suggested Dave Franchi.

'What about "A Tom Bomb"?' said Ben El Harra.

'I don't get it,' said Dean Oldie who didn't seem at all fazed about his sending off.

'A Tom Bomb . . . Atom bomb, geddit now?'

'Nope,' said Deano.

Drew Stilton sat on his own. It was only then

that Thomas recalled that Drew had been the only player not to join in the congratulations after his goal.

Katie Moncrieff was waiting for him by the door of the bar when he came out of the players' dressing room.

'Boring game. Good draw though,' she said.

'Yeah.'

'And a great goal. I really enjoyed that.'

'Thanks.'

'Look, we can't talk here. Do you mind going out to my car?' said Katie. 'It's important.'

'Okay.'

Thomas glanced over his shoulder as they left the bar together to see if anyone was watching them. It annoyed him to see Drew Stilton leering and sticking his tongue out suggestively. To hell with Drew, he thought, I'm not going to let that idiot get to me.

Katie led Thomas to a white Audi Sports soft top in the car park – he was quite impressed. He hadn't passed his test yet because he'd only been seventeen for a few months and somehow there hadn't been much time for lessons – so the BMW 3.5 Convertible that the sponsors had given him had gone to Elaine. When he had his licence he was going to get an open-top Alfa Romeo Sport just like Cosimo's, only white, or perhaps a Saab Convertible. They settled into the front seats of the car and Katie got straight to the point, 'Do you know anything about match-fixing at Sherwood?'

'What?' Thomas was staggered.

'Match-fixing. You know, when you try to fix the result . . .'

'I know what match-fixing is,' said Thomas. 'But you've got to be having me on.'

'No way. The word's out that someone is taking bungs to throw games. It's big money, too.'

'Who would do that?' said Thomas, hardly believing what he was hearing. So Elaine's right, he thought. Katie Moncrieff is just a stupid, sensationalist journo like all the rest of them.

'Have you seen anything suspicious in the past few days or weeks,' asked Katie.

Thomas thought for a moment. 'Nothing. What sort of thing?'

'Any of the team missing easy goals . . . or giving away the ball too easily in front of their own goal? Or seen anyone with a load of cash?'

'Oh, give over. This is Premier League football. Everyone's got loads of cash. Even Dean Oldie can't spend it as fast as he can earn it.'

'I know. And that makes it worse when someone gets extra greedy . . . and bent,' said Katie.

'How did you hear about this?'

'The story started out in the Far East. Hong Kong. There are big gambling rings out there, and one or two people have been making a packet out of betting – especially on the results of Strikers games.'

'That's not evidence.'

'No. But then I got an anonymous message on my voice mail at work. Naming names. And the call came from a phone box at the Sherwood ground.'

'Who were they, these names?'

'I'm not sure I can tell you.'

'So why are you telling me all this anyway? No one's offered me a bung, if that's what you're thinking.'

'Of course not. If I thought they had, we wouldn't be talking to you. I know you're straight. I thought you might help.'

Thomas said nothing.

'It's Sean Pincher and the skipper,' said Katie at last.

'What? Mac? Now I know you're joking.'

'Think about it,' said Katie. 'They're both nearing the end of their careers and they could be looking for a big pay-off before they retire. And along comes Mr Big from the Hong Kong gambling syndicate . . .'

'Only problem with that theory is that Big Mac and Sean are the least bent people on Earth. They're so straight that . . .'

'Think so?'

'I know so. I know them and I'd put everything I've got on them being straight down the line.' Thomas was getting furious.

'Then how . . .' began Katie.

'How should I know? Maybe someone's just setting them up. Someone with a grudge against them, or the club.'

'Maybe. Anyway, Thomas, keep your eyes open. But take care – these people are dangerous.'

*

Back in the players' bar Thomas walked into a big row between Cosimo Lagattello and Sean Pincher, of all people. It wasn't like Sean to get drawn into an argument – he was normally the quietest member of the team and he kept himself to himself. But now he was really angry and worked up about something Cozzie had said.

'You've got a nerve to criticize me for letting in a soft goal,' said Sean. 'You prance about like a big girl's blouse waiting for the ball to come to you. It's time you put in your share of the work instead of standing around like the flaming statue of Eros.'

'Peeg curl's blouse,' said Cozzie in disgust. 'What is thees? I know nothing about ze peeg's blouses. But I know we lose two points for the mistake of the goalie. And everyone know I am genius and, how you say – playbuilder.'

'Playmaker, I think,' said Dean Oldie, who enjoyed stirring things up.

'Playmaker. Don't make me laugh. You're lazy, overweight and a prima donna,' said Sean.

'*Prima donna*,' screeched Cozzie. 'I give you prima donna in ze face.' He spat out a stream of rapid-fire Italian and then stormed out of the bar.

'What's that mean?' said Deano to Thomas. Thomas had done Spanish GCSE and he'd discovered that there were a lot of words in Italian that he could understand. Cosimo didn't seem to have any difficulty understanding Spanish either.

'Something about Sean's mother, I think,' said Thomas.

'Not a compliment, then?' said Dean.

'Oh shut it, Deano,' Sean exploded. 'If you hadn't been sent off we might have got three points. When are you going to grow up?' And he too stormed out.

'My word,' said Dean. 'What's got into Pinchy? He's turning into a psychopath.' Then he grinned his six-tooth grin and said, 'And I should know.'

CHAPTER FOUR

ON THE SPOT

After the City game the Premier League looked like this:

	Played	Won	Drawn	Lost	For	Against	Points
St James	25	15	5	5	57	19	50
West Thames Wanderers	26	13	6	7	49	20	45
Mersey City	25	12	9	4	42	18	45
Border Town	25	13	5	7	48	20	44
Highfield Rovers	24	11	8	5	46	29	41
White Hart United	24	11	7	6	37	28	40
Barbican	26	11	6	9	46	29	39
Wednesfield Royals	24	11	6	7	25	22	39
Danebridge Forest	24	9	8	7	32	32	35
Kingstown Academy	25	8	9	8	30	32	33
Sherwood Strikers	**25**	**8**	**7**	**10**	**33**	**32**	**31**
Branston Town	24	8	6	10	29	34	30
Mersey United	25	8	6	11	24	36	30
West Vale	25	7	6	12	20	33	27

Alexandra Park	24	7	6	11	19	34	27
Southdown United	25	6	9	10	24	40	27
Weirdale Harriers	24	6	7	11	26	39	25
Fenland Rangers	24	5	8	11	23	48	23
Burton Athletic	25	4	11	10	21	51	23
Sultan Palace	25	2	9	14	18	53	15

Sherwood were still eleventh in the table and already their chances of qualifying for Europe next season were looking remote. In fact, a relegation struggle was beginning to seem more likely. The fans were disillusioned by the lack of success and getting more and more restless. Everyone knew that the next few weeks were going to be make or break for Joss Morecombe and his team. They had three big games in the league coming up – at home against the league leaders, St James, followed by Border Town and then away to Southdown United, relegation strugglers who had been having a good run lately to lift them off the bottom of the table. After that Strikers had an FA Cup game at either Border Town or Second Division, Newlynn City. Newlynn was Thomas's old club and they'd held Border to a creditable 2–2 draw away in the last round. The replay was still to be played.

And finally, in just four weeks, they had the big one – the first leg of the quarter-final of the UEFA Cup against St Etienne in France. Amazingly, for a team having such an ordinary season, they were still in three cup competitions. So the Strikers still had plenty to play for.

Thomas didn't speak to anyone about what Katie Moncrieff had said. He still didn't believe it could be true, but there was something about her confidence which worried him a lot. Had she told him the whole story? Had any of the other sports journalists picked up on the rumours? Should he talk to Mac or even to the boss? And he kept replaying that soft goal on Saturday – Sean was brilliant at getting behind the ball; his timing was his trademark – that was why, at the age of 33, he was still first choice in goal for England. It just wasn't like him to miss a relatively easy one like that. Could he have let it in on purpose? Thomas immediately dismissed the idea as crazy. Sean was as straight as they come and everyone has an off day from time to time.

Thomas relived all the games he'd played in and watched that season. There had been plenty of matches that they'd lost or drawn when they should have won – but he couldn't think of another single incident when Sean had missed an easy save or Mac had shown less than 100 per cent commitment. It was all nonsense. And yet, try as he did, Thomas couldn't get the business out of his head.

Katie didn't help; she kept ringing him at home and leaving messages on his mobile answerphone. After three calls one evening Elaine got really annoyed and said she'd ring Katie's editor in the morning and get her warned off. It was all Thomas could do to dissuade her. But, to tell the truth, Thomas was beginning to dread the phone calls himself. Katie could be so persistent.

'Are you sure you haven't seen either of them talking to strangers at the club?' she asked, having tracked him down on his mobile which he'd left turned on by mistake.

'Positive.'

'You would tell me, wouldn't you?'

'Yeah.'

'Listen, you can trust me, Thomas. Really. I mean, I trust you.'

'Why shouldn't you?'

And so it went on until Thomas was not only getting fed up; he was reaching the point where he was getting suspicious of Katie herself and her role in all this.

At training on Tuesday, Sean complained of a knee problem and after about half an hour he went off to see the physio. Mac didn't seem to have his heart in it either. He was usually the keenest trainer in the game, crazy about fitness levels – but today he just went through the motions – or so it seemed to Thomas.

Old Doolally seemed to think so too. Len was a respecter of no one if he thought they were slacking and he was soon laying into Mac. 'What did you get up to last night, Skip?' he said. 'It's no use to me if you come along here half asleep. I'm counting on you to set an example to the young lads.'

Jamie grunted a few words that Thomas didn't understand and ran off. After an hour's fitness training and practising a couple of set-pieces, Len got them working on close ball control. He had a thing about close skills – 'comfort on the ball' he called it. And, for half an hour he had Thomas taking a long pass, bringing the ball under control and turning his defender in one move. The defender was Dean Oldie, and Thomas soon realized why Dean was one of the most feared defenders in the game. He was all over you, a frantic tangle of elbows and shoulders and pushes and pulls. It was just about legal but you could see that, in the competitiveness of a game, Dean could easily overstep the mark. He never gave up. Just when you thought you were past him a foot would come between your legs and scoop the ball away or there would be a little tug of the shirt when you were off balance. And his language was disgusting. As you went up for the ball he'd do anything to break your concentration – swear, grab your shorts, burst out laughing – and then he'd give you a mostly toothless but disarming smile as he scuttled away with the ball.

'You're stronger than I thought,' said Dean to Thomas in the dressing room immediately after the session. 'But you're a bit predictable.'

'What do you mean?'

'Not all defenders are as stupid as me,' he said with a grin that displayed the six teeth he still had left. 'They learn their forwards proper. Keep a record of them up here.' He tapped the side of his head. 'And I'd say a good defender would have you down as pacy but a bit obvious. You've got to learn to mix it up.'

'How?'

'Well, for instance, you always jump at the same time and try and beat your marker in the air and then go straight past him. That's good sometimes. But don't do it always. Leave your jump till late one time; hold the ball up another. Keep your man guessing. Defenders hate that.' He slapped Thomas on the back and went off for his shower.

A moment later Jason Le Braz came into the team dressing room and saw Thomas. 'Hey, Tommo, you heard the news?'

'News?' Thomas's heart sank. 'What news?'

'You're picked for England B against America next week.'

Thomas felt a surge of excitement run through him. 'What! I don't believe it. How do you know?'

'The boss told me. Drew Stilton's in the side too.'

'And you?'

'Not yet. But they're bound to recognize real talent one day,' said Jason with a laugh. Thomas could tell he was disappointed but he wasn't going to spoil his friend's moment of triumph by showing it. The game was a friendly against the USA. There were two American squads coming over to play against England. The seniors were playing at Wembley on Wednesday night, the B team the previous evening at the Stadium of the North, St James's new ground. It meant that all Premiership games were cancelled at the weekend.

Playing for England – for the national squad – was Thomas's dream. Since his dad was Scottish and his mum from the West Indies, Thomas was also qualified to play for Scotland and the up-and-coming Jamaican side. He'd been quite tempted by an offer when he was at Newlynn City to play for the 'Reggae Boyz' but in the end he'd turned them down. He'd also refused an invitation to play for Scotland's Under-19s because he'd always dreamt of playing for England. And now his chance had come. It wasn't the big one yet – but if he turned it on for the Bs he knew he had a chance of breaking into the first-team squad in time for the World Cup campaign.

'Rory's playing in goal for America B,' said Jason.

'That gives me a fair chance of scoring,' said Thomas with a laugh. 'All you've got to say to Rory is, "Look, there's a hamburger," and then push the ball the other side of him.'

Rory Betts was the number two keeper for the Strikers. He was nineteen – two years older than Thomas – and he too had joined Sherwood at the beginning of the season. Rory was one of those people who seem a lot older than they are because they've done everything. He'd travelled to nearly every country in the world, he was a brilliant guitarist and a computer freak – and, in his spare time – he loved painting. Rory's great weakness was hamburgers; he ate at least six of them a day but he never put on any weight. In spite of his talents, it never occurred to anyone to be jealous of Rory; no one disliked him – apart from idiots like Drew Stilton. And, of course, he was a top-class goalkeeper.

As soon as he'd changed Thomas went to look

for Rory but there was no sign of him so he went back to the car park to get a lift home. He usually got a lift to and from practice sessions with Rory or Jason, or sometimes Ashleigh Coltrane – the practice ground was five miles out of Sherwood.

There was the usual handful of fans, mostly girls, gathered by the entrance to the car park and Thomas signed a couple of autograph books and answered some silly questions about his favourite band and what clothes he liked. One of the girls said she liked hip hop too, and asked him to go out with her. There was a lot of giggling and Thomas felt slightly embarrassed. Then suddenly his attention was caught by a small group of people standing by Jamie MacLachlan's Merc. Mac was one of them and Sean was there, too. But who were the other two men? They were both wearing expensive suits – a big guy with a beard who looked like a bouncer, and a small man in black who stood with his back to Thomas. As Thomas watched he shook hands with Mac and Sean and then turned and walked away from them. He was Chinese or Japanese. Katie's words immediately rang in his ears – '. . . along comes Mr Big from the Hong Kong gambling syndicate . . .' This wasn't Mr Big – more like Mr Small. Apart from the owners and waiters at the Chinese restaurants, you didn't often see a Chinese person in Sherwood. And Thomas got the feeling Sean and Mac weren't ordering a takeaway. So what was going on?

CHAPTER FIVE

ENGLAND DEBUT

When Thomas ran out of the tunnel in his England B shirt it was the first time in a week that the Sean and Mac business hadn't been on his mind.

It had been a very long week. He'd decided not to talk to Katie or anyone else about what he'd seen in the car park. He'd wanted to tell Elaine but he thought she'd only laugh at him. After all he didn't have anything to go on – seeing two of his team-mates with a Chinese person wasn't exactly evidence of a link with the Hong Kong mafia. But somehow he was beginning to believe the worst.

Hoping to pick up some further scrap of information he followed Mac and Sean around after training all week until he was sure they were getting suspicious of him. He even tried asking Mac about his business interests but that got him nowhere either.

'Youz wannae kip yer beeg nooz oota waat disney consirn yee, wee Tommeh,' Mac said gruffly. And Thomas left it at that – he hadn't understood a word but even so he got the message.

Then on Friday he saw Sean on the phone. He looked really shifty. Thomas crept closer to hear what he was saying: '. . . Yes, Ma. Yes, we're all coming over on Sunday. Young Brendan wants to show you his new tractor,' Sean was saying. And Thomas sidled off, feeling even worse about his suspicions.

There was no question about it – this match-fixing mystery was beginning to obsess him. But, when he heard the roar of the crowd in the Stadium of the North, he forgot about everything but playing for his country. To be honest, the crowd wasn't that big. He'd played in front of more people at Newlynn City, let alone at Sherwood. But running out for England B meant more to Thomas than anything he'd done before in his life. What would playing for England in a World Cup be like, he wondered.

There were three Sherwood players in the England B starting line-up – Drew Stilton, Dave Franchi and Thomas himself. Rory Betts was in goal for the opposition. And in tomorrow's first team friendly Sean Pincher and Ashleigh Coltrane were playing for England and Brad Trainor for the USA. A total of seven players from Sherwood Strikers were getting a run out in the two international games. It was just as well there had been no Premier League games at the weekend.

England won the toss and Thomas got his first

feel of the ball when Graham Deek, who was making his third B team appearance, passed back to him from the centre spot. Thomas immediately made an early run at the US defence but was well tackled. He was a little annoyed with himself for giving up possession so easily.

Dave Franchi had an even more disastrous start. His early clearance went straight to the feet of the American skipper who lofted a beautifully weighted pass into the path of their lone striker. He chested it down and hit it in one movement. It was a wonderful piece of skill and the England keeper had no chance – all he could do was pick the ball out of the back of the net and curse Dave Franchi for his carelessness. There had been a suggestion of offside but the assistant ref's flag stayed down and the referee pointed to the centre spot. England B were one goal down only six minutes into the game.

The crowd got quieter. After half an hour of deadlocked football with America defending solidly and getting everyone behind the ball, the England B coach made a substitution. The number three was limping after a heavy tackle and the coach brought on a midfield player to replace the defender and pushed Graham Deek further forward, alongside Drew Stilton. The new 4–4–2 formation was designed to allow Thomas and the right wing back, Teddy Halliday, to get forward to give the team some width in attack. The idea was that they would break along the wings and provide opportunities for Graham and

Drew to latch onto. Just before half time Thomas got a long, flighted cross-field pass which put him clear down the left touchline. He beat his marker, went for the by-line and looked up. A big defender was bearing down on him; Drew was in the centre and Graham coming in at the far post. Thomas side-stepped the defender and crossed with his right foot. The ball curved over Rory Betts in goal and over the centre back. Deekie met it with a flicked header aimed down and to the keeper's left. Rory dived and got a hand to it – but, unfortunately for him, he succeeded only in pushing the ball into the path of Drew Stilton. Drew picked his spot and, before the tackle came in, he drove hard and low just inside the left post.

Arms outstretched, Drew took off like an aeroplane – he ran for the touchline, ignoring the congratulations of his own players and milking the crowd's applause like an old pro. He loved it. And when the whistle went for half time he was still preening and strutting about. He mocked Rory Betts for dropping the ball at his feet and told Deeky that, if the header had fallen to him, he'd have buried it first time. Not a word of congratulations to Thomas for the cross – but that was typical of Drew. He lived for just one person only – Drew Stilton; he was so in love with himself that he scarcely noticed the existence of anyone else.

The goal just before half time lifted the whole team – to go in at 1–1 was very different from being a goal down – and everyone was talking at once in the dressing room when the coach walked in. Brian Donkins had been at West Vale, Barbican and Mersey United before he got the England B job. Thomas sometimes wondered why they'd given it to a manager who had been sacked by three Premier League teams. As Deekie said, 'He's a patronizing old sod when he's sober and a silly, patronizing old sod when he's drunk.' Sober or drunk, Donkey just loved the sound of his own voice.

'That's more like it, boys. At last we're getting the pace of the game and setting the tempo,' he said. 'What did I say earlier?' He paused for a reply but none came. 'I said it would take a bit of time for you all to feel comfortable on the ball and get the pace of the pitch. Now I want you to go for it. Keep your shape but just push up a bit and force them square by going down the wings. Don't lose your nerve if we don't get a goal immediately. Steady build, patience, move it about in nice triangles and it'll come. Any questions?'

There weren't. In less than a minute Thomas had felt his enthusiasm drift away. He began to realize what effective motivators Joss Morecombe and old Doolally were in comparison to Donkey Donkins.

Coincidence or not, America began the second half strongly and, instead of pushing up, England were pushed back and forced to defend. Dave Franchi made amends for his earlier mistake with a brilliant overhead kick off the goal line and the keeper came to their rescue on three occasions with fine saves, including a brave dive at the feet of the Americans' goalscorer whom Thomas had marked down as the most dangerous and skilful player on either side.

Then there was a sudden break at the other end and Drew was clean through on his own with only Rory to beat. He shot way over the bar. As he walked back Thomas couldn't resist saying something. 'Were you trying to lob him or knock his head off?' he asked Drew.

Drew scowled. 'What do you know about anything? It hit a divot, that's all. You saying you could have done better?'

'Couldn't have done much worse.'

'Don't make me laugh. If you were any slower you'd be going backwards.'

Thomas shrugged and left it at that. Perhaps he shouldn't have said anything – but it was too tempting to wind Drew up whenever you got the chance – he was so unbearable and arrogant the rest of the time.

About half way through the second half all the pressure coming from the American team suddenly seemed to evaporate. For no reason at all they appeared to lose their rhythm and Thomas and the England midfield began to link up with Deekie and Drew up front again. A long throw-in from the far side allowed Thomas to go on a searching, diagonal run across the American box. A quick one-two with Deekie stretched the defence still further and left a hole for Drew to run into. Thomas spotted him immediately and curled a low short cross just in front of him. Drew took off. His header would have knocked Rory off his feet if he'd been anywhere near it. Instead the keeper could only watch as it drilled into the back of the net.

Drew was starting off on another glory run when he saw the assistant referee's flag raised and heard the ref blow for offside.

'Offside, you must be effing joking,' he shouted at the ref.

'Don't push your luck, son,' said the ref grimly. This wasn't a ref with a sense of humour and if Drew couldn't spot that it was his funeral. 'Another word out of you and you're off. Understood?' he said.

'But how could that be offside? There were two defenders between me and the goal,' persisted Drew. 'That stupid git must be blind.' And he swore again – this time worse than the first time.

'I'm warning you,' said the ref.

Deekie tried to pull Drew away but he wrestled free and turned on the referee again. 'That was a goal and if you can't see it you can both get stuffed,' he screamed. With his face screwed up in anger and pushed so close to the ref's for an awful moment Thomas thought he was going to head-butt him. The red card was just a formality now. Drew saw it, scowled and walked off without another word – spitting on the ground as he went. He's going to remember his first game in an England shirt, thought Thomas . . . and so is the England coach.

There were twenty minutes to play and, with England down to ten men, they had to reform and rely on breakaway attacks. A draw looked more and more likely. The USA team fortunately didn't find its full rhythm again and the match became a bit scrappy. Thomas got the feeling that the American lads were tiring a bit – perhaps some of them weren't as match-fit as the English players. He decided to test it out with a couple of runs down the wing and on the second occasion he got past his marker and put in a good deep cross that reached Deekie at the far post.

Thomas, following his cross in, saw Deekie head the ball back, aiming for one of the England midfield trio bearing down on the goal. The shot was way off target but one of the American defenders went for a panicky clearance and sliced the ball across the goal to Thomas. It was a lucky break but Thomas didn't need two invitations. He volleyed it with his right foot into the roof of the net from just five yards out.

'Well at least we got a result. Even if it took a fluke of a goal to do it,' said Graham Deek after the game.

'Fluke?' said Thomas. 'It was pure skill keeping that volley down.'

'But I bet their full back's feeling pretty sick for gifting it to you.'

'Got young Drew off the hook anyway,' said Dave Franchi.

Everyone turned to look at Drew who was

sitting on his own sulking. He hadn't said a word till now. 'What yer mean?' he snarled at Dave.

'I mean you lose your rag and get sent off – and you nearly cost us the game. And if you ask me a spoilt brat is a luxury we can't afford.'

'And if you ask me . . .' mimicked Drew. 'Listen, Dave, everyone knows it's time you were giving rides at the seaside.'

Dave Franchi clenched his fists and went red in the face but Deekie put his hand on his shoulder. 'Come on, Dave – we won, didn't we? Let's enjoy it. Time to celebrate.'

CHAPTER SIX

BACK TO EARTH

After the England B game Thomas found he was once again, the centre of attention. There wasn't a journalist in the whole country, it seemed, who didn't want to interview him, talk to him, take photos of him or buy him lunch. Elaine had all her work cut out keeping them at a distance – and even she didn't succeed all the time.

One morning when he was just starting his cornflakes, Thomas spotted a photographer taking pictures of him through the window from the garden. A couple of days later a ridiculous story appeared in the *Comet*: Thomas – it claimed – was going out with a supermodel called Minouche. There was the picture of Thomas eating his cornflakes and alongside it one of him and Minouche getting into a car and a string of quotes from people who had seen them together in hotels and clubs 'holding hands' and 'looking dreamily into each other's eyes'. All of it was news to Thomas – not only had he never met anyone called Minouche but he'd never seen her or heard of her. He couldn't believe it. The picture was a fake; the stories all made up. It made him feel sick and he almost began to think that he couldn't trust his own memory.

Katie rang him the morning the article appeared and asked him why he hadn't given her the story and, when he told her it was all made up, she muttered, 'I can't believe what scum some journalists can be.' Thomas wasn't convinced. He was beginning to think she was as bad as all the others. Once again she asked if he'd seen anything strange at Strikers, but Thomas kept his thoughts to himself. Usually he loved reading about himself in the papers but he wasn't really in the mood to talk to anyone from the press at that moment – including Katie.

Meanwhile to make matters worse, the Strikers' fortunes on the pitch were plunging. It wasn't so much that they were playing badly but they were just not getting the breaks. Two more defeats in the league had left them dangerously close to the relegation zone. They lost unluckily by a late goal – the only one of the game – against St James, and then they were on the wrong end of a 3–4 home result against Border Town. It was a game they should have won after being 2–1 up with a quarter of an hour to play but then everything went mad. They allowed Border to up the tempo and completely lost their shape at the back. As the defence collapsed they leaked three more goals to go 2–4 down and then Ashleigh scored a consolation goal on the final whistle. '£75 MILLION STRIKERS CRASH AGAIN!' screamed the headline in the *Mirror*, above Katie's scathing review of the game.

Worse was to come – the grumbling fan revolt against Joss Morecombe started to grow again. A lot of people were saying that he'd taken a huge gamble with his young players and, as it wasn't paying off, it was time for him to go. It wasn't just the supporters who were complaining either. An interview with Frankie Burger appeared in the *Post*. It was a nasty, bad-tempered piece in which Frankie claimed he'd asked to be put on the transfer list because he'd lost all faith in the manager and he felt the skipper was well past his sell-by date too. He also hinted that Sherwood was doing some dodgy deals in the transfer market – from which his interviewer concluded that he was talking about the signings of Thomas and Rory Betts. Everyone at the club knew it was sour grapes. Frankie hadn't asked for a move – he'd been pushed.

Then there was another turn up – Frankie denied the whole thing. He claimed the entire interview was a fiction made up by the journalist and he was going to sue the *Post*. Thomas didn't know what to believe. Frankie was a loud-mouth and it would be typical of him to try and get his own back on Joss Morecombe for pushing him out. But he just wasn't clever enough to play a double game like this. Maybe someone else was behind the story.

The unpleasant atmosphere spread to the dressing room.

'Eetsa grande sbaglio. 'Ow you say? Cock up?' moaned Cosimo Lagattello after the home game with Border Town. 'I no wanta giocare con bambini.'

'What's he say, Tommy?' said Dean Oldie who took a special pleasure in deciphering Cosimo's curious mix of English and Italian.

'I think he said he doesn't want to have any babies,' said Thomas uncertainly.

'Yes . . . babies.' Cozzie pointed at Thomas and Jason.

'Very wise, Cozzie old mate,' said Dean. 'But didn't your dear old Italian mama ever tell you . . .'

'I no come from Italy. I Sicilian,' said Cosimo, sticking out his chest proudly.

'Makes no difference, mate. Even Sicilian men don't have babies. You ask the Godfather.'

'Veree funnee,' said Cosimo. 'But I say "giocare con bambini" – how you say? Pray?'

'You pray all you want, Cozzie; we need all the help we can get with this team.'

'I think he means play – as in "football",' said Thomas. 'I expect giocare means to play.'

Cosimo nodded and slapped Thomas on the back. 'One day you *play* with the beeg boys quando you is un poco piu vecchio. Too much babies righta now.'

'Well thanks, Cosimo,' said Thomas. 'But if you don't mind I think I'll listen to the boss not you. If he thinks we're old enough and good enough to play for Sherwood – then that's fair enough for me.' Thomas felt the anger surge up inside him. He'd heard just about enough about the Morecombe Babes from the media. Too young, too inexperienced, they said, but it was worse to hear it from one of your own team-mates, particularly Cozzie, who swanned around like a tourist half the time, waiting for the ball to come to him.

Dean Oldie rested his hand on Thomas's shoulder. 'You take no notice. He's only jealous,' he said.

'What ees jealous?' asked Cosimo.

'In Spanish it's geloso,' said Thomas.

'Come? Me geloso?' Thomas thought Cosimo was going to explode as he broke into a torrent of indecipherable Italian and then stalked out of the dressing room.

'Funny these Sicilians,' said Deano with a smile. 'They insult you and it makes them angry. But I tell you, matey, being young is nothing to worry about – especially when you've got a talent like yours.'

Dean Oldie wasn't over-generous with his compliments – so that meant a lot to Thomas.

The following Saturday – on the morning of Sherwood's away game at Southdown United – the story at last broke in the press.

'Match-fixing shakes Sherwood' ran the *Telegraph*'s back-page headline. 'Sick Strikers!' screamed the *Post*, alongside pictures of Jamie

MacLachlan and Sean Pincher. The pair stood accused of the crime of selling themselves and their team down the river for big cash deals with a 'murky far-eastern betting syndicate'.

Sean and Mac hadn't travelled on the team coach to Southdown. Thomas saw them both only briefly before the game; they were deep in conversation with Joss Morecombe and the club chairman, Monty Windsor. The reaction in the dressing room was shock and disbelief. No one believed the story apart from Cosimo and Kevin Wardle.

'It's ridiculous,' said Dean Oldie, who was playing his last game for Sherwood for three weeks. His four-match ban for being sent off began with the FA Cup game on Saturday. 'Why would Mac and Sean want to wreck their lives with a fiddle like that? They've made enough dosh out of the game without going bent.'

'If there's anyone less bent than Mac in the world it's Sean,' said Dave Franchi. 'I wouldn't mind getting my hands on the evil creeps who are spreading this rubbish.'

'But it says here they've got evidence,' said Kevin. He read from the *Post*, ' ". . . these amazing pictures are the final proof that MacLachlan and Pincher, once the pride of their countries, have sunk to taking bribes." It says they're going to publish them on Monday.'

'Pictures? Oh yeah, that makes all the difference,' laughed Deano. 'Tell Tommy here about pictures. They can do what they like with computers these days. Stick heads on the wrong body, take your clothes off. What are they going to show us? Sean and Big Mac receiving a giant cheque from the lucky winners of the Chinese football pools?'

'Then why have two papers come out with the same story?' asked Kevin.

'Obvious, matey,' said Deano. 'Someone's trying to stitch up Pinchy and Mac and they've pulled the wool over the eyes of a couple of sad idiots from the national press who can't be bothered to check their facts and would both sell their grannies for a story.'

'I say you no have the fire without the fuming,' said Cosimo. His English was improving – but not by much.

Thomas thought of Katie. There had been nothing in the *Mirror*. He wondered how she would feel when she read this. He didn't have to wait long to find out. Katie was covering the game and she saw Thomas walking through the supporters' lounge. She rushed over immediately.

'You've seen the papers?'

'Yeah. But there was nothing in the *Mirror*.'

'Tell me about it. I'm in deep schtuck with the editor. He wants to know why I missed out on the biggest scandal to hit football since the Jock Graham bungs story. And, when I told him I already knew about it, he hit the the roof. I probably won't have a job on Monday. I just didn't think there was enough hard evidence.'

'Well, those other two aren't quite as fussy as

you are. Do you still think Sean and Mac are guilty?' asked Thomas.

'I dunno. Sean's let in some soft goals lately for Sherwood. And he was brilliant in the England game. Look at that goal against Rovers – it isn't like him to time his dive so badly. And the one at St James looked a bit dodgy to me too.'

Thomas felt rather sorry for Katie. She had been straight with the club after all, he thought. And, before he knew it, he'd told her about seeing Sean and Mac with the little Chinese man.

'Why didn't you tell me this earlier?' asked Katie.

'It didn't seem that important,' lied Thomas.

Katie thought for a moment and then she said, 'I want to talk to Mac and Sean.'

'You and the rest of the world's press,' said Thomas.

'But you know I'll be fair. I'll hear them out.'

'Maybe. But it'll take a bit to convince Mac and Sean.'

'Then you'll have to persuade them for me.'

'Me?'

'Yes. It's their best chance . . . if they're innocent. The papers are going to be full of the match-fixing story all week. They'll be tried, and if the *Post*'s pictures are convincing enough, they'll be found guilty before they have a chance to tell their own version. Unless they talk to me.'

'Why should they listen to me?'

'If they don't, it's their funeral. But it's worth a try, isn't it?'

'Okay,' said Thomas, wondering precisely what he was letting himself in for.

The game itself was a fiasco. Mac got a knock early on but he struggled on till half time when Joss Morecombe took him off. By then Strikers were a goal down thanks to another mistake by the keeper. Sean came out for a cross, missed the ball completely and Southdown's number nine headed into an empty goal. Sean was struggling to keep his mind on the game; he must have been shattered by the press stories. But he had to play because Joss didn't have a reserve keeper available; Rory had flu and the third-string keeper had been concussed in his last game with the reserves. So Sean had to struggle on.

Sherwood began the second half with a makeshift midfield of Cosimo and Thomas in the centre and Jason and Kevin Wardle, who had come on for Sean, playing outside them. The 4–4–2 set-up usually suited Strikers well, but it was alarming how much they missed Big Mac's authority in the centre. Then Ashleigh Coltrane got an ankle injury – he was clattered to the deck by Southdown's big central defender when he seemed to have a clear run on goal. It should have been a red card but the player got away with a booking and Curtis Cropper came on for Ashleigh. Curtis wasn't used to playing the lone front role and, as he dropped further and further back, the midfield became even more congested.

Even so, Jason and Drew both missed clear chances on goal and Strikers were beginning to press hard for the equalizer when a Southdown break resulted in a stunning goal – a blistering twenty-yard drive which grazed the inside of the post. This time Sean was not to blame – the shot was unstoppable. After that a few heads went down and a third goal to Southdown came in injury time after a messy goal-mouth scramble.

0–3 against Southdown United was the worst result of a none too brilliant season for Strikers. Joss Morecombe summed it up in the dressing room after the game. 'That,' he said, 'was the pits. But when you reach the bottom of the pit there's only one way for you to go. Up. And that's where we're going.'

Thomas was grateful to Joss. He could have really slagged them off for the way they'd played. But Joss was too experienced a manager to do that. The whole team's confidence had taken a battering from the match-fixing story and it was Joss's job to build it up again.

As the table now showed, Strikers were heading rapidly towards a relegation dog-fight.

	Played	Won	Drawn	Lost	For	Against	Points
St James	28	17	6	5	61	20	57
Mersey City	28	13	11	4	47	19	50
West Thames Wanderers	28	14	6	8	51	23	48
Border Town	26	14	5	7	52	23	47
Highfield Rovers	27	13	8	6	51	31	47
White Hart United	27	12	8	7	39	30	44
Wednesfield Royals	26	11	8	7	26	23	41
Barbican	28	11	6	11	46	33	39
Danebridge Forest	26	10	8	8	33	36	38
Mersey United	27	10	6	11	27	37	36
Kingstown Academy	28	8	11	9	31	37	35
Southdown United	28	8	10	10	30	42	34
Sherwood Strikers	**28**	**8**	**7**	**13**	**36**	**40**	**31**
Branston Town	27	8	7	12	30	37	31
Alexandra Park	26	8	6	12	20	35	30
Weirdale Harriers	27	7	8	12	29	41	29
Burton Athletic	27	6	11	10	27	51	29
West Vale	27	7	7	13	21	36	28
Fenland Rangers	27	5	9	13	25	53	24
Sultan Palace	28	2	12	14	20	55	18

CHAPTER SEVEN

UP FOR THE CUP

The line up for the FA Cup game – away to Newlynn City – contained only five players from the Sherwood Strikers team of less than a month ago. The latest casualties were Dean Oldie (suspended), Cosimo Lagattello (sick), Jamie MacLachlan (knee injury) and Sean Pincher, who had asked to be rested for a week. Dean Oldie said Sean had gone to see his family in Ireland to get away from the press.

Mac and Sean had both been under enormous pressure. The so-called match-fixing photos appeared in the *Post* on Monday. They really weren't that convincing. There were shots of Sean and Mac talking to, and then taking a large brief-case from, a small man who the paper said was an agent specialising in transfer deals and who had shady connections with the Hong Kong under-world. Both players had claimed they had never seen the character in the picture before, let alone talked to him.

'I'm sure Mac hasn't got a tie like that,' said Ben

El Harra when they met up for training on Monday morning.

'It's just as Deano said,' added Ashley Coltrane. 'Someone has fixed these on a PC.'

'Seems very likely to me,' said Rory Betts, who was Strikers' high-tech freak. 'I could do it easy.'

'I'd like to see you try,' sneered Kevin Wardle.

'What? Fit up a picture like that? Dead easy,' said Rory.

'Can you do one for me?' asked Deano. 'Perhaps I can stitch up that ref who sent me off on Saturday. Maybe one of him in a blonde wig and a little, tight skirt?'

As the week wore on the newspaper stories got more and more outrageous. Big Mac's home was under siege by the press – up to twenty of them were camped day and night outside his front door. One story claimed that his injury was a complete sham and he was just too yellow to face the music. That was rubbish. Thomas had seen Mac's left knee after the Southdown game; the bruising was severe and the doc had told him to rest it for ten days. He didn't train all week but he came along to watch the practice sessions from the touchline – he said it was better than staying at home with the media goons.

Cozzie, on the other hand, had done a runner. He claimed he was sick – suffering from food poisoning after the Indian meal they'd all had last Saturday night – Cozzie loved complaining about the food in England. It was a bit strange that no one else had fallen ill after the meal . . . although not that strange because Cozzie had a reputation for doing a 'sickie'. Deano, who picked up all the gossip, said that he'd put money on Cozzie having done a disappearing trick, particularly since his Italian girlfriend had come over earlier in the week. The boss was furious and he announced that, unless Cosimo returned with a very good excuse, he was suspended for two games and, if it happened again, he was out for good.

As the week progressed the match-fixing stories got sillier and sillier – there were even wild accusations that more than half the team was involved. On Thursday Joss Morecombe was forced to call a press conference. He told a packed room of journalists – most of whom Thomas had never seen before – that the club was holding its own investigation as well as cooperating with the police. He said that, until there was concrete evidence against them, Sean and Mac had the full support of the club and would continue to play.

Katie Moncrieff was there and when Joss took questions she asked him whether he'd had any reason to believe that Sean and Mac were not 100 per cent committed to the club.

'Not for a moment,' said Joss. 'I've known Mac for nearly ten years and Sean since I joined Sherwood and, as far as I'm concerned, they are both model pros.'

So what did he personally think of the allegations?

'Complete twaddle and rot,' said Joss. 'And I

hope you'll all print that.' It was a good performance. Katie thought so, at least.

'I'm beginning to feel there's something funny about all this,' she said to Thomas after the press conference. 'I've tried to find out more about that little guy in the pictures. You know, the agent who's supposed to have given them the money.'

'And?'

'He seems to have vanished. At least I haven't met anyone who has done any business with him for well over a year. A lot of the managers know him but they say that he hasn't been on the scene at all lately – not for months. And I checked out your Chinese businessman. You'll never guess who he is.'

'Who?'

'He's one of the top people at Children in Need and he was talking to Sean and Mac about a big charity match they've agreed to help with.'

'I know about that; I'm playing in it,' said Thomas, feeling suddenly ashamed of all his suspicions. 'You didn't tell anyone else that I . . .'

'Of course not. What do you take me for? What are the other players saying?'

Thomas told her that everyone seemed convinced that Sean and Mac were innocent – except perhaps Kevin Wardle and Cozzie Lagattello, and Cozzie probably hadn't understood what was going on in the first place and wouldn't be interested if he had. Then he told her about Deano's theory about the photographs and what Rory had said.

'Interesting,' said Katie. 'Maybe I'd better have a word with Rory.'

Newlynn City had got through to the fourth round of the Cup after a surprise win in the replay with Border Town. Thomas had mixed feelings about playing against his old club. It would be nice to see some of his mates from last season but, at the same time, he was expecting a hostile reception from the City supporters. They hadn't been too impressed when he'd signed for Sherwood. That was just part of the downside of being a soccer star – the fans thought they owned you and they could go from loving you to hating you overnight. Thomas got a handful of really nasty abusive letters when he signed for Sherwood. He was upset about them for weeks. Even though the other players told him that it went with the territory, it didn't make it easier to ignore the abuse. Joss told him there were a few nutters who thought that sport let them off decent behaviour and they didn't belong to civilization.

The Cup tie kicked off at 3.00 pm. The Newlynn crowd didn't give Thomas too bad a time after all – there were a few boos from the regulars at the Harbour end as he ran out and his first touch of the ball was met with a big, ironic cheer. The City supporters were in a good mood – expecting an upset. Given Sherwood's recent problems and their dreadful results, a lot of money was going on a win for the underdogs. There was no shortage of jokes, of course, about the betting scandal.

'Where's Big Mac gone?
Gone to put his money on,'
chanted the home crowd.

And when they got bored with that, they started another:

'Pincher, Pincher
You're bent, int cher?'

Sean hadn't come to the game and Mac wisely stayed in the dressing room.

It didn't take long for Sherwood to realize that they had a real contest on their hands. Newlynn were up for this one all right. Thomas was clattered to the ground twice in the opening minutes as the Newlynn fans roared their team on. There were almost as many Sherwood supporters as home fans in the ground but they certainly hadn't found their voices yet. After five minutes Dave Franchi, who was stand-in captain, went up for a high ball and there was a nasty clash of heads. He suffered a cut over his eye and seemed a bit concussed so Joss replaced him with Ezal Delmonty, the Turkish international, and Ashleigh Coltrane took over the skipper's arm band.

The Newlynn City pitch was even worse than Thomas remembered it. The surface was patchy and the ground was a bit boggy down the left-hand side. It was a perfect giant-killers' pitch because it forced the Strikers into errors; they were mistiming their passes, giving away the ball and letting City into the game.

Even so, Sherwood were looking the more

likely to score when, just before half time, they were hit by a sucker punch. Newlynn threaded a ball through which beat Strikers offside trap. Ezal Delmonty had been a bit slow to react and he played the City striker on. The shot from twenty yards beat Rory and hit the post. The rebound fell to the feet of Gary O'Casey, Newlynn's top goalscorer. He dummied a shot and then cut inside Ben El Harra who lunged at the ball. His tackle was a fraction late but it looked worse than it was because Gary let out a piercing cry, did two somersaults and lay face down as if he'd been shot. He'd always been a bit of an actor, Thomas remembered. The ref had no doubt, though; he pointed to the spot. O'Casey revived immediately, took the penalty and tucked it away in the bottom left by the post, sending Rory the wrong way. The whole City crowd leapt up with a deafening roar of delight – but in the area behind the goal no one moved. The Sherwood supporters sat fixed in their seats in silent disbelief.

Half time was a gloomy affair in the Sherwood dressing room. They were losing the winning habit and there didn't seem to be much they could do about it. Joss said a few words of encouragement and Big Mac had a long talk with Ashleigh Coltrane in the corner of the changing room.

'We're going to hit them hard – right from the restart,' said Ashleigh to Thomas. 'I want you to play up with me and Drew, and I've told Ben to get down the wing whenever he can. But make sure you're back to cover the breaks. There'll be gaps at the back and they'll try to take advantage of them. Remember, it's not just a Cup tie, it's the most important game of football you've ever played in your life. So give it all you've got. We need a win.' He hesitated for a moment, and then he added with a determined look, 'And so let's go out and get one – for Sean and Big Mac.'

The second half began at a furious pace with Sherwood laying siege to the Newlynn City goal, but it began to look look as if the gods were not on their side. Jason hit the crossbar and Drew got a yellow card for diving when there seemed little doubt that he'd been brought down in the area. For once he didn't overreact – maybe getting sent off in the England game had taught him a lesson. Then Ashleigh and Kevin Wardle both went close with headers; Kevin's effort brought a brilliant fingertip save from the Newlynn goalkeeper.

Time was running out when Thomas sent over yet another cross and Drew Stilton rose above the defence and headed the ball to the feet of Ashleigh Coltrane. Ashleigh hit it first time, sliding the ball under the diving keeper. There was a momentary silence – and then, at last, the Sherwood supporters came to life with a mighty roar. The chanting got louder and louder and two minutes later their optimism was rewarded. Brad Trainor delivered an inch-perfect pass for Drew Stilton to run on to. He rounded the full back and then angled his shot just inside the far post. Sherwood were in the lead. Thomas didn't have a lot of respect for Drew as a human being, but his footballing talent wasn't in dispute. As he watched Drew run the length of the pitch towards the delirious Sherwood supporters, he remembered what Joss Morecombe had said to him – 'it takes all sorts to make a football team'. Drew had his disciplinary next week for the sending off in the England game. He'd probably be suspended – and Thomas knew that his skills would be missed.

Urged on by Ashleigh, Sherwood didn't sit back on their lead but kept taking the game to Newlynn. There was one nasty moment when, with Rory way off his goal line, Gary O'Casey tried to lob him from fully forty yards, but the ball just carried over the bar. At the final whistle Thomas was booed off by some of the City crowd – but he didn't mind. 1–2 was a good result in a tough, fiercely contested tie. Maybe he was on his way to his first FA Cup winner's medal. And maybe Strikers were on the long road back.

CHAPTER EIGHT

FRENCH CONNECTION

After Saturday's gruelling game, Joss Morecombe had virtually no time to prepare for the UEFA Cup quarter-final against St Etienne on Wednesday. Drew Stilton's disciplinary earned him a three match ban but fortunately it didn't start until the following Saturday. That meant he could play in Europe and, as Joss was struggling to put any kind of team together, that was an enormous relief. Sean was still away and Joss wouldn't go back on his decision to drop Cosimo even if it meant turning up with ten men and the mascot. He might have forgiven him if he had apologized for Saturday but the Italian didn't understand the meaning of 'sorry'. He turned up for training on Monday as if nothing had happened and when Joss asked him where he'd been he just said airily, 'So – Cosimo wasa occupato – how you say, bisee.'

'Well I hope Cosimo is bisee on Wednesday night because he no play football in Europe.' Joss was very angry but he wasn't going to give Cosimo the satisfaction of seeing it.

Cozzie couldn't believe what he was hearing. 'Ees a joke, no?'

'No.'

Cozzie stamped his foot, then he pleaded, charmed, tore at his hair and stamped the other foot. He begged and he shouted and he waved his arms about, but it cut no ice with the boss. He told Cozzie to come back when he could behave like an adult, and kicked him out.

After Cozzie had slammed the door Joss read out the team for the UEFA Cup game. Cozzie's name was out, of course – but there was an even bigger surprise. Frankie Burger was back in the squad. Joss hadn't been particularly happy about naming Frankie, but he had little choice – there was simply no one else fit or experienced enough for the big game. Jamie MacLachlan was back, too – but only if he passed a fitness test. However, out went Dave Franchi and Curtis Cropper who'd both taken knocks on Saturday – neither of them were going on the trip.

Later that day, after the hubbub of the airport and an hour-and-a-half flight, the team were in their hotel in St Etienne. Surprisingly, Frankie was as good as gold. He was sharing a room in the hotel with Kevin Wardle and he seemed really pleased to be playing again, in spite of all the things he'd said about Joss and the Sherwood set-up. Thomas shared with Jason and Rory got the short straw – Drew Stilton was his room-mate.

'He spends all his time looking in the mirror and combing his hair,' said Rory, taking refuge later that evening in Thomas's and Jason's room. 'I don't think he knows I'm there. It's a bit creepy really – I feel like a ghost.'

There was a gentle tap on the door. Jason opened it to see Katie Moncrieff.

'How did you get in here?' said Jason as Katie stepped into the room.

'Never mind how. I am here.' Katie turned to Thomas. 'And I've got something to show you. It might be important but then again it's probably not. I had an e-mail from my boss at the *Mirror*; it's a bit weird.'

Katie put her lap-top computer on the table and called up her e-mail. The message read:

> Received note for you left with reception. It reads, 'Keeper and Skip didn't do it. Try Number Ten.' Probably some nutter – no signature, no identification.

'What can it mean?' asked Katie. 'Number Ten?'

'Search me. Your editor's probably right. Just a loony. It always happens when there's a big story in the press,' said Rory.

'Do you think it means Number Ten Downing Street? You know, the Prime Minster's home?' said Jason.

Katie shrugged. 'But it doesn't make sense. What on Earth can the Prime Minister have to do with this?'

'He's a big St James United supporter, isn't he?' said Thomas.

'Yes. But I don't think he's so keen that he'd get into fixing games at Sherwood – just to help St James win the Premiership,' said Katie with a chuckle.

'I didn't mean that, stupid,' said Thomas crossly.

'Perhaps we should ring him,' suggested Jason.

'Who?'

'The PM.'

'Oh yeah. Good idea. We could invite him round for a few beers and a kick about,' said Rory. 'Make a day of it and tell him to bring the wife and kids.'

'Na. He wouldn't come, would he?' said Jason who wasn't very quick at spotting sarcasm.

'Well, let me know if you think of anything,' said Katie. 'I can't stop – I've got to write something about your chances in the big game on Wednesday. It's hard to think of anything positive to say.'

'Oh yeah?' said Rory. 'Lucky for us then that you journalists know nothing.'

Katie laughed. 'Oh by the way, thanks for fixing up that interview with Mac, Thomas. It's in the paper tomorrow. I think he'll like it,' and with that she left, leaving Thomas more puzzled than ever.

*

'Skip looks fit enough to me,' said Len Dallal to Joss Morecombe as they stood watching the Strikers' last practice session before the big game.

'He's fit all right. But is he mentally up to it?' said Joss.

'Don't worry about that – Skip's tough as they come. He'll pull through,' said Doolally.

'Let's hope you're right. We're stuffed without his experience. I feel as if I'm managing the Under-15s sometimes.'

'The young lads won't let you down either,' said Len. 'I'll bet you Strikers win tomorrow night.'

'You know I'm not a betting man. So why don't you get down the bookies and put some of your money on it for a change,' Joss replied.

'Maybe I will. I wonder what odds I'll get for 5–0?' The old coach had a dreamy look in his eye.

'5–0! Now I know you're losing it, Len.'

Len shrugged and wandered onto the practice pitch to shout at Jason, who was leaning up against the goal post talking to Rory.

Len's language got a bit exotic during training. He swore like a trooper and told everyone exactly what he thought of them if they were slacking. After directing a torrent of abuse at Rory and Jason, he called everyone round him.

'Right, I want to go over those corners we practised last week,' he said, gathering everyone round him. 'These St Etienne boys are flashy footballers but they're mostly on the short side. So what we do is this . . .'

They practised three variations on their regular corners. And then they practised them again and again . . . and again. Len was nothing if not a perfectionist. 'Jason, lad – I want you to run forward off the near post and take your marker with you at exactly the same time that Kevin makes his run. The corner then floats to the near post. Number ten heads it back and Skip and number nine run on to it.'

As he listened a strange feeling came over Thomas Headley. Suddenly he understood everything. It didn't seem possible – but the more he thought about it, the more he knew he was right. He could hardly wait to talk to Katie. He looked over to the touchline, where along with the rest of the press pack, she was watching Sherwood practise. Her interview with Big Mac had been very fair – she had almost proclaimed that the match-fixing charges were a joke. And Mac had seemed to cheer up a bit when he read the article.

As soon as the training session ended Thomas jogged over to talk to her. 'I've got something to tell you,' he said.

'What?' asked Katie.

'Number ten. I know what it means,' said Thomas.

Katie stopped dead and looked hard at him. She pulled him to one side, out of earshot of the other journalists. 'What did you say?'

'Well I might be wrong . . .' continued Thomas.

'Oh, do us a favour, Thomas. Spit it out, will you?'

'Well . . .' began Thomas. 'Who's the one person in the team who thinks Mac and Sean are guilty?'

'I dunno. Wait, didn't you say something about Kevin Wardle and . . .'

'And what number does Kevin have on his shirt?'

'Number ten.' As she said it, her eyes widened.

'Try number ten . . .' said Thomas slowly.

Katie stared at him. 'Wait a minute – you're not suggesting Kevin knows something about this?'

'Maybe . . . and there's another thing I thought of,' said Thomas. 'Only one person calls Big Mac "Skip", and Pinchy "Keeper" – and that's old Doolally.'

'You're saying that Len Dallal sent that message, and . . .'

'And he thinks Kevin Wardle knows more about all this than he's letting on.'

Katie was silent for a moment, then she said, 'Kevin and Frankie Burger are pretty close, aren't they?'

'Sort of,' said Thomas. 'Kevin's a big mate of Frankie's brother, Dez. Aren't they sort of in business together?'

'Yes! They own Burgers Club. And it isn't just the club Dez Burger owns. He's got his fingers into loads of things: restaurants, casinos, betting shops . . . you name it.'

'Betting, eh?' said Thomas.

They looked at each other, excitedly.

'So what can we do about it?'

'You can do nothing,' said Katie. 'The only thing you're going to think about is winning a football match.'

'But . . .'

'I need to talk to Rory . . .' said Katie half to herself. Then she abruptly changed the subject. 'Did you know that Len's putting £20 on Sherwood to beat St Etienne 5–0?'

'5–0 away from home? He's off his trolley.'

'Well, the odds are 150–1. So if he wins he picks up £3,000.'

CHAPTER NINE

ALL BETS ARE OFF

The match began at 7.00 pm – 8.00 pm British time. It was televised live across Europe and, thanks to the invasion of over 10,000 Sherwood fans, it was a complete sell-out. There had been just a spot of bother in the bars of St Etienne during the afternoon and ten English fans were arrested. Strikers' supporters usually had a good reputation – not like West Thames Wanderers – but every team had a hard core of hooligans following them around. According to Katie the French police had gone a bit over the top in making arrests. By the time the kick-off came round, the stadium was bristling with police in riot gear.

As Big Mac led the Strikers out, their supporters rose to give them a champions' reception. By comparison the French crowd was relatively quiet, apart from the bangers and firecrackers which seemed to be a local tradition.

The pitch was perfect. It had been watered a couple of hours before the game, so the ball came off it lightning-fast and the surface was as smooth as an ice rink. Joss began the game again with a 4–4–1–1 formation, with Ashley up front and Thomas on the left of midfield. He preferred playing up front or in the centre but he was quite happy on the left as long as he could play an attacking role down the wing. This was the line-up:

22
Rory Betts

21 Jason Le Braz | 4 Brad Trainor | 14 Tarquin Kelly | 3 Ben El Harra

10 Kevin Wardle | 12 Frankie Burger | 6 Jamie MacLachlan | 7 Thomas Headley

20
Drew Stilton

9
Ashleigh Coltrane

Apart from the reserve goalkeeper, Joss had only four substitution options on the bench: Ezal Delmonty, who'd had an ordinary game against Newlynn City; midfielder Paul Bosch and two forwards, Lanny McEwan and the Swiss striker, Aaron Bjorn Rorschach (pronounced Raw Shark) who had just come back from injury and scored a hat trick in his last game for the reserves.

The St Etienne boys looked sharp in the warm-up. They'd had a much better season than Sherwood and were currently second in the

French first division, just behind Marseille. They also had three players in the French national squad – so no one was underestimating the danger.

The ref was German. He spoke to the players in English and French. His English was good – but the French players seemed to have some difficulty understanding him. He got the match under way dead on time and in the first minute St Etienne were very nearly ahead. A series of half-clearances by the Sherwood defence led to the ball eventually floating out to a St Etienne midfielder. He threaded a perfect pass through to Ricard, the French danger man up front. Ricard ran onto it and hit a rocket of a shot from fully thirty yards which Rory couldn't get a hand to. It hit the underside of the crossbar and bounced back in play just on the right side of the goal line. Rory collected as Ricard ran in to challenge him.

This early success put a spring into the feet of the St Etienne players and for twenty minutes the Strikers struggled under immense pressure. Brad Trainor timed a perfect tackle as Ricard ran on to a dangerous cross; then they hit the upright and Rory made two more reaction saves. It seemed just a matter of time before the French would go ahead.

In the twenty-second minute, after another breathless near miss by the St Etienne forwards, Ben El Harra cleared up field to Ashleigh Coltrane. Turning his marker he was fouled but he managed to stay on his feet and the referee waved play on. Ashleigh laid the ball out to Thomas on the left and he scampered down the wing. His curling cross was met by Drew Stilton's right-footed volley which found its target under the diving goalkeeper.

St Etienne didn't panic. Instead they continued to dominate and their patient build-ups gained them a free kick in the D just outside the penalty area – Tarquin Kelly's late tackle earned him the first yellow card of the game. The French protested that he'd committed the foul inside the box but were told by the German referee in very firm English – he seemed to have given up on his French – that he was running the game and, if anyone argued with him again, he would be sent off. That seemed to do the trick. Ricard bent the kick over the wall and the dipping ball was destined for the top left-hand corner of the net when Rory pulled off the save of the night and fingertipped it over the bar. It was a nearly impossible reaction save, as he could have only seen the ball in the last split second, and yet he covered half the width of the goal to touch the ball over. Ricard couldn't believe it.

The corner came across, whipped in from the right, and Rory sprang to take the ball off Ricard's head. 'I no like this English goal guardian,' said Ricard, picking himself up.

'Hey, I'm not English, I'm American,' said Rory.

'But nobody play football in America,' said Ricard. 'Only American football and basketball.'

'Well I've got news for you, buddy. The

Americans are coming,' said Rory. 'We'll meet again in the World Cup, maybe.'

'And maybe I score a goal past you before that,' said Ricard.

'We'll see,' said Rory with a smile.

The French pressure didn't let up at all but the Strikers defence held out. Just before half time Brad Trainor picked up a yellow card for another late tackle – this time on Ricard.

'Hey, guy. Sorry,' said Brad casually as he pulled Ricard to his feet.

'You American too?' said the shaken Frenchman.

'You betcha.'

'These Americans are everywheres. They save my brilliant free kicks – then they kick me up in the sky,' muttered Ricard, rubbing his shin. 'Americans go home.'

At half time Joss was over the moon. 'If we can hang on to the lead in the away leg we're an odds-on bet for the semi-finals,' he said. 'I'm not changing the formation because I want to keep the attacking options and not get too compressed at the back. So Ashleigh stays up with Drew playing off him. Try and mix it up – first a long ball, then play it across the field, then passing triangles and, when they're least expecting it, run at them. You're all playing brilliant. I've a feeling we're going to get a result here.'

The second half began with an amazing sequence of play. Jason, who had slotted brilliantly into the back four, executed a perfect tackle on one of the French forwards – hooking the ball away to deprive him of a clear shot on goal. He did a quick one-two with Brad and then took off down the right. Frankie Burger was screaming for it in the middle but Jason switched the play to the left with a pin-point pass to Thomas who was hugging the touchline. Thomas saw that Ashleigh was just onside and poised to run onto the ball. He sent in a fast curling cross and Ashleigh met it with his head just by the penalty spot. The ball spun off his head, downwards towards the bottom right-hand corner of the goal. The goalie dived, got a hand to it and deflected it on to the inside of the post. As the ball ran back across the goal, Ashleigh, who had continued his run, met it at full stretch and slid it into the net.

Ashleigh picked himself up as Drew, Mac and Frankie followed him into the French goal, and he was buried under a tide of hugs and congratulations. 'Trane, yerra wee beauty,' exclaimed Mac, his face lit up with the biggest grin he'd shown in weeks.

The Sherwood supporters went barmy. 0–2 was beyond their wildest dreams and now they really were in the holiday mood. The French fans, on the other hand, had gone very quiet indeed. St Etienne made a double substitution, pushing more players forward in a do-or-die attempt to get a goal back or even two. They almost succeeded when Ricard lobbed Rory as he came off his line. But he then watched in disbelief as the ball bounced off the top of the crossbar and went behind for a goal kick. 'I never play against Americans again,' he muttered. It wasn't his night.

With ten minutes to go, Ashleigh Coltrane ran diagonally across the pitch towards the French goal. He beat one defender and was then brought down by their sweeper just inside the area. Firing from the penalty spot, Ashleigh made no mistake – sending the goalie the wrong way. St Etienne 0 Sherwood Strikers 3. Two minutes later, with the French committed to all-out attack, Jamie MacLachlan won a tackle and put Ashleigh clean through the middle with a beautifully weighted pass. He carried the ball twenty yards, dummied a shot, went round the goalkeeper and slotted it into the net from the left-hand side. He celebrated his hat trick with a Coltrane shuffle at the corner flag in front of the delirious English supporters.

At 0–4 with only a couple of minutes of normal time to go, old Doolally was living up to his nick-name. He was running the length of the field along the touchline as if he was warming up to come on. Every now and again he would jump up in the air and wave a piece of paper – shouting out the name of one or other of the Sherwood players.

'It's his betting slip,' said Ashleigh to Thomas. 'He's one goal away from three thousand quid. Let's see what we can do for the old fool, shall we?'

Ashleigh had a word with Big Mac and Jason pushed forward to make it three up front. The

French were now in disarray – not knowing whether to attack or defend. Their supporters were already leaving in droves – jeered at by the Strikers fans from behind their goal. Sherwood won a throw on the halfway line. Ben El Harra took it and received a return pass from Frankie Burger. He sprinted down the wing and then back-heeled to Thomas who sent in a first-time cross from fairly deep. It was too close to the goal-keeper, who should have caught it. But instead he ran out and half-flapped, half-punched at the ball. It fell to the feet of Kevin Wardle, just outside the area. Kevin feigned to shoot with his right foot and then tucked the ball inside to Frankie Burger who was bearing down on the goal like an express train. He unleashed a kick of such power that, although the keeper got his hands to it, the ball burst through them into the back of the net. The ref blew for the goal and then blew again for the end of the game.

It was party time behind the goal and on the pitch. As he exchanged shirts with a speechless French midfield player, Thomas looked across the pitch to the dug-out. Even Joss was dancing about, celebrating and hugging everyone who came near him – including the poor St Etienne players and their manager. Never can a team have dominated a game for so long and ended up at the wrong end of a 5–0 scoreline. They just didn't know what had hit them.

But alone on the Striker's bench, one figure did not move. He had his head in his hands and he was motionless. Old Doolally could not believe it. He had just won £3,000. But it wasn't the money he was thinking about – at least not directly. He had won it thanks to a goal by Frankie Burger, laid on by Kevin Wardle. Only Len knew the true irony of that. Or so he thought.

CHAPTER TEN

FINAL SCORE

ST ETIENNE 0			**SHERWOOD STRIKERS 5**		
			Stilton (25) Coltrane (48, 79, 85)		
(Half time 0–1)			Burger (90)		
		Rating			Rating
1	Briffa	6	22	Betts	8
3	Colombani	5	4	Trainor	7
4	Benamou	6	14	Kelly	7
5	Costa	5	21	Le Braz	8
14	Mistinguet	7	3	El Harra	8
6	Gavroche	8	10	Wardle	7
8	Distel	5	12	Burger	7
11	Sharpe	6	6	MacLachlan	8
12	Trebucher	6	7	Headley	9
9	Ricard	9	20	Stilton	8
10	Lapetite	7	**9**	**Coltrane**	**10 MOM**
Reserves					
2	Frederic	-	19	Delmonty	-
7	Saint Rupert	6	17	Bosch	-
18	Laculotte	6	24	McEwan	-
23	Lapaz	-	23	Rorschach	-
15	Hourani	5			

Attendance: 50,000

Referee: H. Schwarzkopf

Thomas loved statistics. For him the ratings tables were the best thing on the sports pages. It was always the page he turned to first – although he hardly ever thought they got it right. Today there was no arguing, though. Ashleigh, with his first hat trick this season, had to be man of the match. And Thomas wasn't going to complain about being voted the second best player on the pitch.

Some of the other players, Ben El Harra and Sean Pincher for instance, said they never read the newspapers because they were full of rubbish. Thomas didn't go along with that. He read every sentence – rubbish or not – written about Sherwood Strikers and Newlynn City and, especially, anything about himself. Katie had said a week or two back – before the match-rigging business had come up – that she wanted to do a profile on him. She hadn't mentioned it again and Thomas was wondering whether it was too egotistical of him to remind her about it.

The English morning papers, which the team glimpsed at Lyons' airport on their way home, were a pleasure to read. For the first time in ages they had something nice to say about Sherwood. There was nothing like beating the French to get a good press in the tabloids. The headline writers were in ecstasy and went completely over the top. 'STRIKERS BLITZ FRENCH CHAMPS', 'Un, deux, trois, quatre, SANK', 'AU REVOIR!', 'COLTRANE'S FRENCH LESSON'. Katie's article in the *Mirror* was headed: 'STRIKERS DREAM

ON' with a picture of Ashleigh sliding his first goal into the St Etienne net. And then another story caught Thomas's eye – it was just a little piece in bold type alongside the main match report and it read:

MacLachlan and Pincher innocent

The *Mirror* knows for a fact that Sherwood Strikers' captain and keeper are completely innocent. The charges of match-rigging are a lie and completely trumped up. How do we know?

Read the full, amazing story tomorrow only in the *Mirror* – first with the sports news.

'Hey look at this,' said Thomas, pushing his paper in front of Jason Le Braz. 'What's Katie up to?'

'Why don't you ask her,' said Jason. 'She's over there.'

Thomas hadn't been the first person to spot the piece. There was a buzz of excitement amongst the press pack and Katie was besieged by a small group of journalists who were demanding to know where the story had come from. Suddenly she spotted Thomas and ran over to him.

'I want to talk to you,' she said. 'Quick. Follow me.'

She raced across the departure lounge before the pursuing journalists knew what was happening. Thomas couldn't believe how fast she moved – he could hardly keep up with her and he was supposed to be one of the quickest footballers in the country. They turned a corner and he followed her through a door marked *Défense d'Entrer* and into a little room with tables and chairs laid out like a small classroom.

'How did you learn to run like that?' gasped Thomas.

'You're looking at the Scottish Under-18s 200-metre champion" said Katie.

Thomas was impressed. He looked around. 'Where are we?'

'How should I know?' Katie put an ear to the door. 'Good. I don't think anyone has followed us. Now listen – have you seen Kevin and Frankie this morning?'

'Yeah. I saw them at breakfast in the hotel and on the coach, I think.'

'And at the airport?'

'Well – no.' Thomas was losing patience. 'Listen. What's all this about?'

'All right. But I can trust you to keep it to yourself, can't I?' Thomas nodded and Katie sat down on one of the chairs and began her story. She told him how she and Rory had set a trap for Kevin after the game. Rory had taken one of the pictures of Sean and Mac from the *Post* and, on computer, replaced their heads with those of Kevin Wardle and Frankie Burger. Katie had taken photographs of both of them before the match.

'Rory did a really good job,' said Katie. 'It was just as convincing as the *Post*'s original pictures. We left it on the table in Kevin and Frankie's room . . . Rory picked the lock. He's got hidden talents, that boy.'

'But why?' asked Thomas, completely baffled.

'I suppose he gets it from his parents,' said Katie.

'No, I mean why did you do all that and leave the picture in their room?'

'Because I wanted to hear what they'd say. We bugged the room, too.'

'Bugged the room? I don't believe you.'

'It was Rory's idea. He said it was really easy. And it is. You don't even need wires or anything. You just stick this little black thing in an electric plug. Mind you it costs a bomb, but my editor didn't mind paying.'

'So what did they say?' Thomas was beginning to think he'd stepped into a Russian spy thriller.

'Listen to this.' Katie pulled a little tape-recorder out of her brief-case and pressed the 'Play' button. Thomas recognized Frankie Burger's voice immediately.

Frankie: *I told you this wasn't going to work, Kev! Someone's on to us.*

Kevin: *Don't be stupid. Relax. No one can prove*

we've got anything to do with it. It's just some idiot's idea of a stupid joke. I bet I know who's behind this.

Frankie: *Who?*

Kevin: *Our Yank pal, Rory Betts.*

Frankie: *I don't like it.*

Kevin: *Don't tell me that now.*

Frankie: *I didn't want to get Sean and Mac involved in this from the start.*

Kevin: *We had it all agreed, didn't we? Things were getting too hot for me and you and your fat, greedy brother.*

Frankie: *Don't talk about Dez like that. I'm warning you . . .*

Katie stopped the tape player. 'There's lots more like that.'

'What does it mean?' asked Thomas.

'It means Sean and Mac were framed. The real match-fixing duo were Kevin and Frankie. It was them, together with Frankie's brother, Dez, who made up the story for the press.'

'And sent those pictures to the *Post*?'

'Yes.'

'But why?'

'The way I read it is this. The winnings in the Far East were getting too big. People started talking about match-fixing. Remember my informer from Hong Kong? So Kevin and Frankie got nervous. It was probably Dez's idea to frame two innocent players. He planted the stories with Kevin's help – Frankie's not bright enough to get up to anything like that. Kevin's always been jealous of Big Mac's success so he was the obvious target. They were trying to put up a smoke screen. If you muddy the waters enough, it can make the truth impossible to get at.'

'How long do you think they've been doing it? Fixing games?'

'Not long. Just this season is my guess.'

'And their scheme nearly worked. A lot of people fell for it.'

'But not Len Dallal, luckily.'

'How do you think Len got to the truth?' asked Thomas.

'Because he watches. He doesn't miss a thing that goes on during a game. Haven't you noticed? He writes all the moves down in a funny sort of code he has. He can recreate any match. And he spotted things in the pattern of play. I spoke to him first thing this morning. He's been wondering about Kev and Frankie for weeks.'

'Why didn't he go to the police? Or the boss?'

'Because he didn't have any real proof. Just a hunch. So he sent that note to me, and then you realized where it came from – and that's how we got on to the scent of Kevin and Frankie. It strikes me old Len deserves that £3,000 payoff from the bookies.'

Thomas sighed. 'What happens next? Is it all going to come out in tomorrow's *Mirror*?'

'Not all of it. I won't mention Len or you or Rory.'

'Just pretend it was all your own idea?'

She grinned at him. 'Sort of. But the police will want to know everything.'

'The police?'

'Of course. It's a serious crime – what Kevin and Frankie have done. Two serious crimes even: fixing games for money and also framing innocent people. They'll probably go to prison if they're convicted.'

'And what's going to happen to Sherwood Strikers? I suppose the press will be hanging round for months.'

' 'Fraid so. But it's better that the truth's out. Joss and the board can start building up the club's reputation again. You've got a great team and the only way to show 'em is on the pitch.' Katie smiled at Thomas and then looked at her watch. 'I've got to go and file my story.'

She moved towards the door and then stopped as Thomas said quietly, 'Katie, do you ever get fed up with your job?'

'Often,' said Katie. 'I can't stand newspapers, and editors, and some of the other hacks – but there is one thing that keeps me going.'

'What's that?'

'Football. I love everything about it. Watching it, talking about it and, above all, writing about it. So I'm pretty lucky really.'

'I guess it's the same with me,' said Thomas with a broad smile.

'There one difference – you don't write about it, you play it. I wish I could do that.'

*

Kevin Wardle and Frankie Burger turned up again in Sherwood a few days later. They insisted they were innocent and they were both suspended on full pay by the club. The trial took over a year to come to court and when it did the jury decided the evidence was insufficient to convict them.

By this time both of them had left Sherwood to join teams in the lower divisions. Neither of them ever played another game in the Premier League and both their careers went rapidly downhill. Frankie's brother, Dez, was forced to sell up his businesses and leave town, too. And that was the last Thomas saw of any of them.

RESULTS

Week 1 – Tuesday

Sherwood Strikers 2	Highfield Rovers 1	League Cup

Week 2 – Saturday

Mersey City 1	Sherwood Strikers 1	Premiership

Week 3 – Tuesday

England B 2	United States B 1	Friendly

Week 4 – Saturday

Sherwood Strikers 0	St James 1	Premiership

Week 5 – Monday

Sherwood Strikers 3	Border Town 4	Premiership

Week 6 – Saturday

Southdown United 3	Sherwood Strikers 0	Premiership

Week 7 – Saturday

Newlynn City 1	Sherwood Strikers 2	FA Cup

Wednesday

St Etienne 0	Sherwood Strikers 5	UEFA Cup